MIRANDA'S MUSE

A Novel

By

Arlene Spector

© 2002 by Arlene Spector. All rights reserved.

No part of this book may be reproduced, stored in a retrieval system, or transmitted by any means, electronic, mechanical, photocopying, recording, or otherwise, without written permission from the author.

ISBN: 1-4033-4607-0 (e-book)
ISBN: 1-4033-4608-9 (Paperback)

This book is printed on acid free paper.

Acknowledgments

I would like to thank my husband, Murray Spector for his expert technical editing, his thoughtful criticism, and most of all his patient and loyal support; Anne Bennedsen, for educating me about paganism and The Wicca; Regina O'Melveny for her thoughtful editing and for helping me to coax Miranda onto the written page, and last, but not least, my sister, Joan Colombo for loving me and Miranda.

Arlene Spector
San Pedro, California

Any resemblance of the characters in this book to real persons, living or dead, is purely coincidental. Furthermore, the events depicted herein are fictional and do not represent any true happenings.

A.S.

CHAPTER ONE

Once, in a small town in northern California, a woman named "Miranda" ran a cafe appropriately named "Miranda's Cafe." Most of the people who came to her cafe told themselves that they came for the delicious food she prepared, but it was really her stories that had captured their attention. The words she chose, her remarkable speaking voice, and the tales she had composed completely enthralled them.

"Once," she might begin, "before the earth was even thought of, there was a magic place, loved by the Goddess, where joy and peace, laughter and loving kindness ruled supreme." As she went on describing each flower that grew there and each creature that lived there, her listeners would find their cares dropping away from them like dead leaves in autumn. With each shining word, they would feel a lightness of spirit that transcended even their darkest moods.

Often, Miranda would tell of strange and comical creatures; "The ouroboros is a worm," she would explain, "who has the unique compulsion to swallow his own tail. Thus he spends his entire life going in smaller and smaller circles, devouring himself through all eternity." They chuckled at the impossible picture this created for them, but some felt a little uncomfortable as well; they sensed a subtle message in Miranda's story, if only they were wise enough to understand it.

Sometimes, however, there was a soaring sense of freedom that gave some folks the courage to tackle *seemingly impossible tasks. All at once, they found that they possessed the ability to complete them successfully. The pleasure of this was so uplifting, that they blessed Miranda's soul each time that they prayed.*

The Storysmith
Dos Hermanas, California

Miranda closed the front doors and locked them from the inside. She turned the "closed" sign around so that it would be visible from the street, turned off the lights in the dining room of the cafe and walked back through the swinging doors into the kitchen. The coffee was still hot in the large urn, so she poured herself a cup, added milk and sat down at the large scrubbed wooden table. "I've been alive for more than sixty years now; I am satisfied with the life I have lead. Cooking good food and telling stories brings me great joy. If the Goddess wills it, I'll have many more good years, but no one can predict what she has in store for each of her children. Maybe it would be a good idea to pass these gifts on to a younger person—one who would like to follow in my footsteps." Miranda pondered a while as to how she might find such a person; someone who would want to devote his or her life to the muse. She would have to find a very special person, someone who had "the gift": who would be willing to learn how to run the cafe. It would not be easy. Nevertheless, Miranda felt compelled to try. "Maybe I should sponsor a story telling contest. I wonder if that would work." After mulling it over for a while, Miranda came to a decision. She decided to consult the Goddess.

* * * * * * * * *

As Miranda pulled the small pick-up truck into the driveway, her mind was busy with the unfinished details she would have to take care of the next morning when she opened up the cafe. She pressed the garage door opener clipped to the sun visor and pulled the pick-up carefully into her space. Joseph's sedan was already there. Miranda turned off the ignition and reached for the small spiral notebook she habitually kept on the empty seat beside her, a ballpoint pen conveniently clipped to the page where she had left off writing. As she jotted down all the "to-do's" she had collected during the ride home, she crossed them off in her mind:

1. Call Adler's Farm and order fresh eggs and roasters for the weekend.
2. Find out if Mel and Dan will be available for Saturday and Sunday.
3. Stop at the bank and pick up small bills and change for the cash register.
4. Call Tony and get him over to paint the cafe bathrooms; they're looking dingy.

Finally, when Miranda had exhausted her list of chores, she breathed a big sigh and sat for a moment longer to allow the day's work to drain away. She could feel her sense of wholeness gathering once more around her core. Warmth flooded her body as she opened the door and climbed out. How good it felt to come home, especially when Joseph was already there waiting for her.

She opened the door from the garage into the house and called out, "Hi, I'm home."

"Welcome, stranger!" joked her husband and came to greet her with a warm close hug and a juicy kiss. "I'm just taking dinner out of the oven. Have you eaten?"

"Not really," she replied. "I had some soup at the cafe, but that was just to fend off starvation. Anyway whatever you're cooking smells great!"

Joseph had already set two places at the kitchen table by the time Miranda had washed her hands. She sat down and waited as Joseph sliced his special meat loaf, and beat the mashed potatoes with butter and hot milk.

As she waited for her man to join her at the table, Miranda reflected on the goodness that an early marriage to Joseph had brought to her life. They were in their early twenties and just finishing up their schooling at the university, when they met and fell deeply in love with one another. Each of them had followed a separate career path for a while; Joseph in the world of corporate business management and Miranda as a schoolteacher. They married soon and both continued to work for a while, but when their first child was born, Miranda settled into the role of homemaker and mother, while Joseph continued to rise in the corporate hierarchy. After their third child was born, Miranda realized that she needed to find another career that got her out with people more. Since she had always loved to cook, she enrolled for an eighteen-month course in cooking and restaurant management. Shortly afterward, they decided to move to northern California, where Joseph had accepted a position as an instructor in the business division of the local college. Miranda and Joseph had always been interested in gourmet cooking and Miranda prided herself on having a knack for combining familiar foods in new and interesting ways. So it seemed like a good idea to purchase the old "Dos Hermanas Diner" when the previous owner retired.

Miranda remade the diner into "Miranda's Cafe" and took charge of the day-to-day operations, while Joseph kept the books, took care of the taxes and all the other financial details of running their business. The combination of his work at the college and for the cafe worked out well for both of them.

Each of their three children had completed a university education and was now independent. Two of them had married and in due course presented Joseph and Miranda with five healthy and beautiful grandchildren. Their younger son was struggling to start a business with his girlfriend, but their prospects looked bright and Miranda had no fears for their future.

After the meatloaf, mashed potatoes and fresh steamed broccoli had been consumed, Miranda made a pot of jasmine tea and brought out a fruit bowl. They sat companionably over their tea and picked idly at the grapes decorating the bowl of Jonathan apples, Bosc pears and honey tangerines. They chatted amiably about the events of their day. "I need to finish that paper I'm going to deliver in February," commented Joseph, "so I expect to be working on it most of this evening."

"Oh that's fine, Joseph," Miranda answered, "I've got some serious thinking and meditating to do."

"Anything I can help with?" he offered.

"No, not just yet," she replied. "I need to clarify my own ideas first. Why don't you get started, while I finish up in the kitchen?"

"Good idea," he responded. "That way, maybe I'll get to bed at a decent hour." He rose, kissed Miranda on the top of her head and went off in the direction of his home office.

Miranda placed the teacups and fruit plates in the dishwasher and wiped off the tile counters. Her mind was already busy planning for tonight's ritual. She took the bowl of fruit from the table and removed some empty grape stalks, which had dropped their juicy burden to the bottom of the bowl. Other than that, Miranda thought the fruit bowl looked very inviting, rather like a tromp l'oeuil masterpiece of the Dutch school, where each droplet of water was as perfect as each of the fruits. The only detail missing, she thought wryly, was the tiny black ant which one could usually make out somewhere in the painting as mute testimony to the perfection of the artist's work.

Miranda smiled at the thought as she climbed upon the kitchen stepstool and opened a cabinet somewhat higher than the others. She took out a small-stemmed dish made of exquisite cream-colored porcelain with an elegant gold and cream braided border. She placed it next to the fruit bowl and then went to the refrigerator to take an egg from the carton. She examined it carefully to make sure it had no tiny cracks and then warmed it briefly between her hands. Finally she placed it carefully in the porcelain dish. She stepped back to admire the effect and then stepped slowly out the side door and into the kitchen garden.

Miranda moved quietly from one herb patch to another, selecting a perfect sprig of each variety - parsley, mint, oregano, rosemary, sweet basil and woodruff. She arranged them into a nosegay; both pungent and delicate herbs lent their special gifts to Miranda's bouquet. Evening or early morning was the best time to gather them, before the warm sun could dry the dew. Miranda returned to the kitchen and placed the herbs in a small crystal vase, which she took from a shelf near the window. She set the herbs down with the fruit bowl and egg dish, and stood back once again to admire her "Still Life with Fruits, Egg and Herbs." She felt a warm sense of satisfaction with the beauty of her offering.

As she turned to leave the kitchen, Miranda heard the soft flip-flop of Joseph's house slippers coming from the hallway. She waited for a moment until Joseph came through the doorway into the kitchen, his large blue china mug in hand. As he came toward her, Miranda smiled. The light from the hallway behind him had turned his sparse gray hair into a halo. She chuckled at the idea - Joseph an angel? Not likely! As good-natured as he usually was, Miranda knew it was not a good idea to cross him. He could be as stubborn and difficult as any man, but given their thirty-nine years of living together, each had learned the other's idiosyncrasies well, and respected the boundaries.

"Just coming back for another cuppa tea," Joseph explained. When he saw Miranda's preparations, he smiled. "Well, I guess you and the Goddess have a few things to discuss," he commented as he turned the flame on under the kettle.

"Uh-huh," responded Miranda, "I'll probably tell you about it tomorrow."

Joseph nodded and opened the cupboard to select a tea bag from the canister. Miranda came up behind him and planted a kiss quickly on the nape of his neck. "Watch that, lady," he quipped without turning, "I <u>could</u> be distracted!"

Miranda laughed and ran lightly out of the kitchen and toward the master bedroom.

As she stepped over the threshold, she flipped the light switch. The lamps shed their soft glow on the pale peach walls. The serenity and warmth of their "inner sanctum," as she called it, pleased her. She went into the bathroom and turned on the water for her bath. She threw in a handful of herbal bath crystals and the fresh scent filled the small room. Miranda drew in a deep appreciative breath. She adjusted the temperature of her bath to comfortable warmth and started to strip off her clothing and toss it into the wicker laundry hamper.

When she was naked, she turned and looked at her reflection in the large mirror. What she saw always surprised her a little. It was not that she expected to see a young body. On the contrary, she had always imagined that a woman past sixty would be more wrinkled than Miranda appeared. In fact, time and nature had dealt kindly with her. Miranda supposed that good genes and a healthful lifestyle probably had a lot to do with it. In any case, she liked her body and her face and her hair.

The short curly mass of her silver hair shone under the vanity lights. She couldn't help but wonder what her mother would have thought, seeing her youngest child with such hair, "When did my baby go gray?" would probably have been Momma's first comment. Then, "I like it! Sehr schön!*"

"If only she had lived long enough to see it," she lamented, but the reality of Momma's early demise interrupted Miranda's reverie. "Oh, well, I'm not so sure

---

*"Very pretty"

she really wanted to grow old," she thought and laid her mother's memory to rest.

Certainly, there were very clear indications of Momma's strong genetic influence in Miranda's large brown eyes, her high Slavic cheekbones, her soft generous mouth and stubborn chin. Actually, if one must be honest about it, her plump thighs and ample derriere were also a gift from her mother's side of the family. Miranda's square shoulders, her slender strong arms and capable hands, her wide chest and the very rounded shape of her full breasts must have come from a previous ancestor unknown to her; Miranda had seen no one from either of her parents' families with these attributes.

Her belly reminded Miranda of a road map. A smile-shaped scar low on her abdomen was the sole reminder of her difficult third pregnancy, a Cesarean section; the stretch marks and soft fullness of her belly were souvenirs of the births of her older son and daughter.

The downy thatch of graying hair in the "triangle of Venus" was still a rather sensitive subject for Miranda. Somehow, although it made perfect sense, it had never occurred to her that pubic hair also turns gray as one ages. She remembered clearly the day she had stepped out of the shower and confronted herself in the mirror. She was not wearing her glasses, of course, but even so, something had looked different to Miranda. She had donned her gold-rimmed spectacles and peered at her crotch in the mirror. "Perhaps I didn't get all the soap out," had been her first thought. So she stepped back into the shower stall for another more careful rinse, forgetting to remove her glasses. When Miranda stepped out of the shower for the second time and dried off her glasses, she peered down once again. The evidence was clear.

She put on her bathrobe and immediately called her older sister, Hannah, back in New Jersey.

"Sis," she'd begun, "something awful happened."

"Oh my god, what is it?"

"I'm going gray," Miranda had wailed.

There was a momentary silence.

"What are you talking about? You've been gray for long time already."

"It's not my head I'm talking about," answered Miranda.

"Oh, yes. I see," Hannah replied. "Well…If you think you've got problems, forget it! I went bald."

Miranda laughed out loud at this memory. Then she remembered that her bath was still running and by now, threatening to overflow. She moved quickly and turned the faucet off. Then she dipped her foot in to test the temperature and climbed in. Slowly, she sank down into the perfumed bubbles. The excess water gurgled into the overflow valve. Miranda sighed audibly and allowed her busy day to dissipate in the foamy water.

Her mind began to wander aimlessly, following whatever misty path it encountered. Miranda sank down, down, down until the water covered her hair, her forehead and chin, and then her nose. She was entirely under water in the large claw-footed Victorian bathtub. She had found it at an auction held at an old gold rush ranch house. What a blessing it was to be able to stretch out fully, with all of her under water. Slowly, she rose to the surface once more. She cleared her nose and ears of water and lathered up her hair with shampoo. Sliding down again to rinse her hair, Miranda began to think about the ritual she would engage in later. She stood and stepped out of her bath and put on her thick terry robe. She felt fresh and new once again, as though she had just awakened. She toweled her hair until it no longer dripped and then ran a large toothed comb through her tangled curls.

When she was dry, she went to her closet and selected a simple white linen caftan. She pulled it over her head and let it fall gracefully about her body, hanging loosely from neck to ankles. The long loose sleeves almost covered her hands. From a small satin pouch in her jewelry box, Miranda took an exquisite gold pendant. It was suspended from a thin leather thong and was a miniature figure of a woman with exaggeratedly full hips, a sleek long-waisted body and high pointed breasts. Her head was smooth and sleek and rested on a gracefully elongated neck; the arms were raised in an open circle above her head. Miranda knew her as "Hathor Drawing Down the Moon." She held the little figure between her hands and with closed eyes, she concentrated on it for a few moments. Then she lifted the thong over her head and allowed it to slip gently down until it rested on the fine linen between her breasts.

Miranda went back to the kitchen and took a small damask tablecloth from a drawer. Then she went out the back door into the garden. The moon was not quite full yet. Even so, it lit the garden so that Miranda could see quite clearly. She still remembered planting all the white and yellow flowers so that they would shine by moonlight. The white pebbles she had chosen for the two garden paths which crossed each other at the center, gleamed like alabaster. At the center of the "X" thus formed was a small white stone table. It was round and was flanked by two small identical white stone semicircular benches, one on either side. Miranda spread the damask cloth over the table until all sides were equally draped; then she smoothed the cloth over the dew-damp stone until it clung as close as skin to the tabletop.

Miranda returned to the kitchen and placed the fruit bowl, the egg dish and the herbs on a dark lacquered tray and carried it out to the table she had prepared. She set the tray carefully on a bench and arranged her offering on the table. Finally she was ready to proceed.

She stood as tall and straight as she could, allowing the cool moonlight to permeate her body and mind. Slowly she raised her arms in an open circle above her head. She began to breathe very slowly and deeply. Three times she did this, until she could feel the sweet night air fill every part of her body.

"Eternal Mother," she called softly, "Come to me now. I seek your guidance." The familiar gentle voice responded, "Yes, Miranda I am here." Miranda slowly lowered her arms and held both hands open by her offering. "I have brought these symbols to remind me of you, divine mother, and your daughters. Here is an egg, symbol of springtime and fertility to remind me of Persephone who visits the underworld in winter, but always returns to remind us of the eternal cycle of life. Here are the most beautiful fruits of the season to remember the rich fertility of woman and the earth. They are for Demeter, who weeps for her daughter in winter and comforts her children when they sorrow. Here are the fragrant herbs of healing and seasoning for Hecate, the crone, the wise woman, healer of broken hearts and ailing bodies. I salute you all, my mother, my sister, my grandmother and friend…all of you who are part of me as I am part of you."

"Well spoken, Miranda," spoke the gentle voice. "What do you need?"

"Only counsel, mother."

"Yes, I know of what you speak. I have heard your thoughts and approve of your plan. You will succeed in what you are trying to do, but it will not be in the way you expect."

"Can you be clearer, Goddess?" asked Miranda hopefully.

"It is not necessary," answered the voice, "you have our blessing."

Miranda stood where she was and maintained her erect carriage while she meditated on what had transpired.

* * * * * * * * *

There was a time in Miranda's life when she did not know "The Goddess". She remembered that, as a little girl of four, she had treasured the fairy tales the children's librarian had read to the children who attended the Saturday morning story hour at the library. She wondered if they could be true. How marvelous it would be if they were! How much safer Miranda would feel if she knew there was a fairy godmother, or a guardian angel watching over her and ready to offer advice when she asked for it.

When Miranda turned five, her parents signed her up for Sunday school at their local synagogue. How dry and dull it was, compared to the wonderful tales she heard at the library. The unknowable God of the Old Testament seemed no match for the kindly fairy godmothers, or the goddesses of myth and fable. When Miranda turned seven years old, she asked the Rabbi if she could also become a Rabbi. The answer was, "No, girls don't become rabbis," Rabbi Cohen went on to say, "Girls have a much more important job. It is our women who create a Jewish home and see to it that the children are properly educated in 'yiddishkeit'…And every Friday night, it is the women who light the candles for Shabbat. Just think of it, Mirandala, without you girls, we men couldn't celebrate Shabbat!" Somehow, even as a child, Miranda knew when she was being placated. So, boys could rise to the top, but girls could not! Well, she would show them! From that time on, Miranda refused to learn any Hebrew. The way she thought of it was, "If I can't win, I won't play!"

As she rose through the grades, Miranda found much to admire in Judaism. She adored the bible stories, especially the story of Rebecca at the well and the story of Ruth.

"Wherever you go, I will go. Your people shall be my people and your God shall be my God." How strong and brave Ruth was! Who would not love her?"

The Ten Commandments were good rules and she could easily subscribe to them. Miranda enjoyed the holidays and festivals, especially when she could stay home from school. On the surface, she was a typical Jewish girl. However, in her heart and her prayers, Miranda sought courage and counsel from "The Goddess". In this, she was not alone.

* * * * * * * * *

Joseph was in his study just completing his work. He shut off his computer, stood, stretched and turned off his desk lamp. He padded slowly into the hallway and toward the kitchen, his empty mug in his hand. As he went into the dark kitchen to deposit the mug in the sink, he stopped.

Looking out of the window, he caught sight of Miranda in her white gown standing motionless in the moonlight. Her face was in repose, her eyelids closed, her hands at her sides. As the moonlight bathed her figure in shining light, the silver of her hair gleamed like satin. Her face was softly shadowed and the glow outlined her body in the fine white linen.

"Sometimes," Joseph thought, "we are gifted with the ability to see the familiar as though we had never seen it before." He gazed at his wife and his love for her warmed and suffused his entire body. Miranda appeared to Joseph as the very essence of womanliness, all warmth and full curves, strong and at the same time, gentle. Her full lips were parted as if in a dream and she seemed both regal and heartbreakingly vulnerable at the same time. Joseph wanted to protect her and, as he felt the warmth and tingle of desire begin to course through his body, he wanted to make love to her as never before. He moved slowly to the garden door and slipped out of his house slippers as he stepped into the garden. He waited quietly for Miranda to notice him.

Soon, her eyelashes flickered open and her dark eyes beheld her husband waiting for her. She turned and came to him as if still entranced. He took her hand and kissed it tenderly. Then he pulled her to him and softly kissed her eyelids and then her mouth. Miranda sighed and leaned more closely against him. He kissed her mouth more passionately, tasted her sweet breath and felt her tongue fluttering like a moth on his lips and on his tongue. His hands moved to cradle her full breasts. He bent and kissed her there and there. She sighed softly and raised her hands to hold Joseph's head and stroke it. Slowly, they parted and taking her hand, Joseph led Miranda to their bedroom.

* * * * * * * * *

There was a soft wind blowing off the ocean when Miranda unlocked the doors of the cafe the next morning. Ruthie, her helper, bustled up just as Miranda pushed the door open, stepped over the threshold and sniffed. The inviting aroma of fresh brewed coffee greeted the two women. "Whoever invented the programmable coffee maker deserves a Nobel Prize," commented Miranda. Beyond that, and a slight hint of garlic left over from yesterday's spaghetti sauce, the cafe smelled fresh and clean. The blue and white checkered tablecloths were freshly ironed with a nice sharp crease across the center of each table. The bud vases waited patiently for their sprigs of chrysanthemum, marguerites and deep orange bittersweet berries from the cafe's small garden.

"Good morning, Ruthie. Did you have a good sleep?" Miranda inquired.

"I hit that pillow and never moved 'til mornin'," Ruthie replied.

She poured two thick china mugs of coffee and added cream to her own and milk to Miranda's cup. They sipped their coffee in comfortable silence and then began to prepare for their regular breakfast clientele. Ruthie lit the large gas griddle and set about mixing up some buckwheat pancakes, while Miranda turned the large electric kettle on and filled it with water. She was glad she had purchased one that could be filled by merely turning a built-in faucet rather than having to lift it and carry it back and forth from the sink. She measured out the correct amount of stone ground Irish oatmeal and added some sea salt to the water.

On impulse, she threw in a handful of golden raisins to plump up as the water heated. Then, when it boiled, she added oatmeal and let it cook until it was thick and fragrant. She poured out several small pitchers of cream and set them on a tray, ready to be placed on the counter and tables in the cafe dining room. She opened one of the large refrigerators lined up on the back wall and removed a large pan of uncooked French toast which had been placed in an egg, milk, salt and vanilla batter the previous day so that it would be properly saturated before it was placed on the hot griddle to puff up and brown. The small jugs of real Vermont maple syrup were already in a large pan awaiting a hot water bath to warm them. Miranda loved these little niceties. "It's the small touches that make a big difference," she was fond of saying.

"Ruthie," began Miranda, "I've been thinking…You and I have been running this cafe for a long time and it's been very gratifying the way the townspeople have accepted us into their lives."

"Yes, indeed," agreed Ruthie. "I'd hate to think how dull things would be around here if folks couldn't drop in to pick up lunch or a snack and pass the time of day with friends, or just chatting with us when we have the time to visit with them…not to mention your story telling evenings. They've become a real event here, and our regulars wouldn't miss one unless they were practically on their death beds!"

"Well," continued Miranda, "what would you think of finding someone to take over when you and I no longer feel up to the long hours…sort of a protégé.

Ruthie was silent for a few minutes while she mulled over Miranda's idea. "I guess it would all depend; where would we find someone who loves to tell stories the way you do, and also knows how to cook and run a business? You've spoiled us all, Miranda." They lapsed into silence.

Just then, the back door swung open and a slender young man with curly sand-colored hair, sparkling gray eyes and a broad smile poked his head through the doorway. "Top o' the morning to you, ladies. Hi Miranda. Hi Ruthie," he called out cheerily. As they acknowledged his greeting, he stepped through the doorway and sniffed appreciatively. "That coffee smells great!" He dropped his books on the corner of the kitchen table, selected a mug from the shelf and helped himself to coffee from the urn.

"Have you had breakfast, Danny?" asked Miranda.

"Well I had a piece of toast at home, but some of that oatmeal I smell would sure hit the spot right now." Ruthie took a bowl from the shelf and ladled out a generous serving of the steaming porridge, dropped a pat of butter on top and added some cream. "Brown sugar's in the canister, Danny-boy. I know you like your oatmeal sweet."

"Yes, Ma'am," he replied and scooped out a generous tablespoon of brown sugar which he carefully sprinkled over the cereal in his bowl. Perching himself on a kitchen stool, Danny proceeded to demolish the oatmeal with great and audible enthusiasm. When he was done, he rinsed his bowl and spoon and placed them in the dishwasher.

Miranda envied Danny's ability to eat so much and still remain so slender. It probably had a lot to do with selecting the right parents, she decided, since she knew the Schoenbergs well. Both Irene and Paul were slim, although they relished good food - including the generous application of butter and cream, rich sauces and elegant desserts with lots of whipped cream on top. "Oh, well," she grumbled to herself, "Some folks have all the luck."

"What's happening, ladies?" queried Danny, "Any good gossip?"

"Now you know we never gossip," objected Ruthie.

"That's right," agreed Miranda, "We just discuss current events, although I am hard pressed to tell the difference on occasion." Miranda removed her tongue from her cheek and gave Danny a big wink. "I'm glad you dropped in this morning, Danny. Ruthie and I were just starting to talk over a special project I have in mind and now that you're here I won't have to repeat myself. Are you and Mel coming in this weekend to help out, by the way?"

"Yes. I am, and I'm pretty sure Mel is available too. I'll check with her tonight and let you know. I can use all the hours you can give me, Miranda," he continued, "my textbooks and stuff cost more than I expected."

"Well, if you'll give your book list to Joseph, I know he'll be glad to use his professor's discount and save you a little...I think he gets ten percent off."

"Cool! Every bit helps."

"Now," continued Miranda, "let me share my idea with the two of you and get your thoughts on the subject: I've been thinking about running a contest. It'll be a short story contest. Each contestant will be asked to submit an original short story. Then we'll have a committee read them and select the four or five best stories. The finalists will be invited to present their stories here at the cafe on a Sunday evening. Our patrons will vote on the story they like the best as well as the best storyteller, and the winners will be awarded prizes. So, what d'you think? Will it work?"

Ruthie and Danny sat quietly for a while and thought about Miranda's idea. "I'm hoping that you two will help work out the details. So far, the basic idea is all I've got."

"Why do you want to do this?" asked Danny.

"Well, for several reasons," answered Miranda. "Most simply, I think it'll be fun and that's probably the best reason I can come up with. I also think it will bring more people in for dinner on weekends. You know my story telling evenings seem to draw a lot of our regulars in on Saturday nights, but perhaps some new voices would be welcome too, especially if they're local folks with family and friends around here who would come just to support them. And then, I know a lot of the younger people like to drive into Ft. Bragg for dinner and a movie on weekends. Maybe a contest would persuade them to come to Miranda's instead, especially if some of their friends were performing.

"Well, it's gonna take a lot of planning and even more work," opined Ruthie. Miranda nodded thoughtfully.

Danny sat thinking about Miranda's idea a little longer. Finally, he spoke up, "I've got an idea that might make it easier for us…And it'd be a real help to me. My Marketing professor has assigned the class a term project. Everybody has to design and develop a marketing plan for a small- to medium-sized business. If it's okay with you, I could use this cafe as my project and develop a complete marketing plan, starting with this contest and including all the advertising you'd need to do to make it come off right."

Ruthie and Miranda looked at each other and smiled. "That sounds great, Danny! How long will it take you to work it out and get back to me with at least a rough outline?"

"Suppose I work on it this week and bring in the rough copy when I come in on Saturday? Then you'd have time to go over it and make any necessary changes."

"Yeah, that would work," agreed Miranda.

"Well I'd better get going, then." Danny glanced at his wrist watch and rose from his stool to give Miranda a hug."

"Give my love to your Mom and Dad," she said.

He nodded, "You bet," and then moved quickly around the table toward Ruthie, but she, guessing his intention, scuttled quickly around the table in the other direction.

"Go on with you, lover boy," she giggled," and pick on someone your own age who'd fancy one of your kisses instead of a poor helpless old lady like me!"

"Oh, Ruthie, my one and only true love, when will you say the word that will make me the happiest man on earth?" he teased.

"Right now, you rascal...Get yourself off to school where you belong and don't be bothering an old married lady! She turned to chase him away, flapping her hands at him as he grabbed his books and ran, laughing, out the back door, They could hear the slam of his car door and then he drove off.

The two women resumed their work and were silent. Their utensils clinking against bowls and the scrape of the pancake turner on the hot griddle were the only sounds now. The stillness flowed back into the spot so recently occupied by Danny and filled it up. The cheerful hubbub he had created had left with him. The silence grew thicker with unspoken thoughts, until Miranda smiled and turned to look at Ruthie.

"Thanks," she said to her old friend. "I knew I could depend on your discretion."

"Well, I figured you had a good reason for not mentioning your other purpose in having this contest," responded Ruthie.

"That's true," admitted Miranda, "but it's nothing all that complicated. You see, I'm not sure if the contest will do what I have in mind. Perhaps none of the contestants will be the right person and I'm afraid it would create hard feelings if I didn't choose one of the winners. It's better if we keep that part of things amongst ourselves: you, Joseph and me."

CHAPTER TWO

In the time of the Matriarchs, stories were passed down from mother to daughter of a deity, who cared for the earth and everything on it with great wisdom and strength, but also with great humor and compassion. She was given many names: "Gaia," the earth-mother of The Old Religion; "Ishtar," goddess of the Mesopotamian culture; "Shekhinah," the feminine aspect of the Hebrew God, and "Mary, Mother of Jesus" by many Christians. To this day, there are strong and wise women among us who call on "The Goddess", as She is now known, to guide and sustain them.

The Storysmith

* * * * * * * * *

When Miranda and Joseph had first taken over the cafe, Miranda usually put in a seven-day workweek. After it became clear that the cafe was well on the way to becoming profitable, she allowed herself a day off every week. Ruthie was a "gift" from the previous owner and proved to be not only competent, but flexible as well. She took easily to the ways of her new employers and often offered them valuable suggestions to make the transition easier. It was Ruthie's idea to hire some youngsters from the local college as part-time help. There was always a pool of students who were happy to earn extra money to supplement their scholarships or allowances.

After Miranda and Joseph met Irene and Paul Schoenberg at a faculty get-together at the college, it was just a matter of time before their children, Daniel and Melanie, were old enough to become steady part-time help at the cafe.

When Miranda came up with the idea of telling stories once a week at the cafe, she had chosen Saturdays at five in the evening as a good time to bring people in earlier than they would have come under ordinary circumstances. In order to prepare herself for her story evenings, she began to take Saturdays off until about four in the afternoon. She used the time to get some extra rest and to familiarize herself once more with that evening's selection. Some of the stories she told were stories that she had written, while others were gleaned from various anthologies and magazines which Mrs. Simmons, the head librarian at the Dos Hermanas Public Library put aside for her.

On this particular Saturday, it was almost four o'clock when Miranda arrived at the cafe. Her three helpers were busily preparing for dinner traffic, while also accommodating the occasional patron who wandered in for a piece of pie and a cup of coffee.

"Hello, busy people!" called Miranda cheerfully. "What's happening?"

"Hi, Miranda," chirped Ruthie as she stirred a pot of sauce on the large black restaurant range. "Everything's under control. The pies are baked, the ham and turkey are in the oven and the pot roast is cooked, sliced and gravied."

"Okay, then, I'll prepare the fish. I ordered some nice fresh red snapper; was it delivered?"

"Yes, indeed, just ten minutes ago."

"Red Snapper Vera Cruz it is then…Fast, easy and delicious, if I do say so myself." She opened a drawer and pulled out a large white apron that covered her from neck to ankles. As she tied the ties once around her waist, she continued: "Did the bakery deliver the cakes I ordered?"

"Yes," answered Danny. "The delivery man just brought in three large chocolate cakes, four cheesecakes and two carrot cakes. I'm making room for them in the fridge right now. I checked the ice cream supply and we still have enough chocolate and vanilla, but we're running low on strawberry and coffee. We could probably use more sorbet as well."

"Remind me to order some first thing Monday, will you, Danny?" He nodded and continued working. It was nice that Danny paid attention to these details. His sister Melanie was another story altogether. She was such a reserved young girl that Miranda couldn't help but wonder about her. Melanie's mind often seemed to be far away, although she did her job acceptably. "Where's Mel?" she asked.

"She's in the dining room setting up," replied Danny.

"Okay, I'll find her in a minute…The spaghetti sauce is made, isn't it?"

"Yes, indeed," answered Ruthie, "I started it first thing this morning after breakfast. It's simmering on the back burner."

Miranda lifted the lid of the heavy iron kettle and took a wooden spoon to taste their famous home made spaghetti sauce. It was a recipe that Miranda and Ruthie had developed over the years. After sautéing lots of onions, garlic and mushrooms in olive oil, they browned a generous amount of lean ground beef. Then they added the finest

Italian style canned tomatoes and tomato paste. During the summer, when the sweet basil was at its best in the herb garden, Miranda had prepared a large quantity of pesto sauce and frozen it in ice cube trays. Then she had broken out the cubes of frozen pesto and stored them in a large plastic bag in the freezer. She added a dozen or so cubes to each batch of spaghetti sauce. After adding the right amount of kosher salt, which had no additives to make it bitter, she ground fresh black pepper right into the big iron kettle, along with a teaspoon of anise seeds and one teaspoon of sugar to make the flavors blend. Just before serving, she added a good shake of oregano, so that it would not become bitter through long cooking.

Over the years, Miranda and Ruthie had mixed and tasted, added new ingredients and discarded some of them until they were satisfied that they could not improve upon either the flavor or the consistency, Only the freshest ingredients were used; never any thickeners. Slow cooking in a heavy iron kettle was enough to bring the sauce to just the right consistency. Patrons of Miranda's Cafe were pleased to notice that the sauce clung to the pasta. No matter what the shape, from rotelli to angel hair, the sauce stayed with it and did not end up at the bottom of the dish, like it did at other cafes and restaurants.

As Miranda dipped the spoon into the sauce, she knew exactly how it should taste. If any ingredient had been left out, she immediately knew which one it was. She waited for the spoonful of sauce to cool briefly and then she tasted it. "Perfect," she announced. "Just the way it should be."

Just then Melanie came through the swinging door. She greeted Miranda quietly and went to the linen cabinet for more napkins.

Miranda's Muse

"Hello, Mel, It's good you're back. We missed you last week."

"Yes, I'd have liked to be here, Miranda. School has been keeping me pretty busy lately. I had a presentation to make to my American Lit. class. It was about Willa Cather and I wanted to do a good job on it. So few of the others knew anything about her and I think her writing style is great!"

Miranda was surprised that Mel seemed so willing to engage in conversation tonight. She was usually kind of shy about speaking up. She and Dan both attended the same college where Joseph was a professor. Danny seemed to have been genetically programmed for business administration. From an early age, according to his mother, he was always engaged in some money making scheme. "Thankfully, they were always honest," Irene Schoenberg had commented wryly. From operating a successful lemonade stand when he was five, he had progressed to garage sales for kids, where books and toys exchanged hands at prices his buddies could afford. Then, he had begun dropping in at the convenience store near his school and, without being asked by Dorothy and Joe Carlucci, the store managers, he would pick up a feather duster and dust the shelves, take delivery of the potato chips, clip them carefully to their display stand, and otherwise make himself useful. Finally, Dorothy and Joe had thrown up their hands and told Danny that while they could not legally hire him, they would, unofficially, pay him one dollar an hour for his work. After checking with his parents, he helped out whenever he had time. He saved what he earned for special things that he wanted that were not in the family budget.

His mind seemed to work so quickly, that jokes and puns seemed to bubble out of him, without his even thinking about it. Naturally, he attracted a coterie of admiring friends, and one could usually locate Danny Schoenberg by the laughter of those around him. He participated in a variety of extra-curricular activities, including the school newspaper, the marching band where he played the tuba, and the drama club. School plays often featured Danny as either the juvenile lead or the clown. Unfortunately, his interests did not usually extend to his class work. He managed to squeak by without failing any courses. Teachers were frequently on the phone with Irene, expressing their frustration with Danny, who was so obviously intelligent and, just as obviously, not interested in his schoolwork.

"What motivates your son?" asked Danny's mathematics teacher.

"Do you think I know," queried Irene, "and that I'm keeping it a secret?"

When Irene spoke to Danny about it, he replied, "I don't understand why, when I have clearly shown my teachers that I understand the concepts they are teaching, I have to do the same things over and over again in school and for homework."

When Danny got to college, however, he did much better. The university atmosphere combined with his professor's respect for his independent attitude and his native intelligence freed him to do his best work, and his grades rose quickly to all A's and B's.

Melanie was very different from her twin. She was a sweet child with gentle ways and good manners. Miranda remembered how little Melanie would follow Joseph around with her big brown eyes, which looked even bigger behind her horn rimmed glasses.

"What does she want?" Joseph asked nervously. "She looks like a little owl behind those glasses and she's always watching me."

Miranda didn't know for sure what was going on in little Melanie's mind. She suspected that the child had a "crush" on Joseph, but that she'd probably die of embarrassment if anyone guessed her secret. So, of course, Miranda said nothing about it. Mel had grown up to be a sweet and softly pretty teen-ager, with a head of wavy auburn hair that fell luxuriously around her face to her shoulders. Her complexion was unusual, combining rosy cheeks and lips with a pale coppery tan…"Tawny" was a word that Miranda often thought of when she looked at Melanie. When Mel had reached five feet four inches, she stopped growing and was chagrined to see her brother continue growing until he reached his present height, which was a full head taller than she. The worst part was that he still seemed to be growing, while it was clear that she would probably add no more than a half inch to her height, if her mother's five feet four and one half inches was any indication.

Melanie was a natural student and pulled in good grades all through school. Nevertheless, she worried each time she had to take an exam that she didn't know enough and would fail. She never did, of course.

Unlike Danny, Melanie did not have a large group of friends. She didn't seem to need them, as long as she had one or two really close friends in whom she could confide.

Books were her constant companions, and if she weren't around, one could be sure to find her at the public library, talking to Mrs. Simmons, who always guided her to authors and titles she was sure to enjoy.

Melanie's social life was not nearly so active as her brother's was. She had occasional dates with boys she met in school or through friends. They would attend football games and dances. Melanie enjoyed these activities, most especially dancing, but also seemed quite content to be at home with her family.

"…and with good reason," thought Miranda. With parents as urbane as Paul and Irene, and a brother who was such a comedian, the dinner table conversations were always lively and interesting. Sunday morning brunch, which often included friends of the twins, was quite an event. Fresh bagels or rolls, smoked fish, a variety of cheeses, pickled herring, Irene's special scrambled eggs, fresh fruit and coffee cake or Danish pastries, along with the lively give and take frequently encountered in Jewish families, kept everyone at the table for two or three hours.

As Miranda thought about them, it seemed nothing short of miraculous that two such different individuals could have co-existed peacefully as "womb-mates." She smiled as she fantasized two little fetuses talking it over and coming to terms with each other as they swam around in their watery world. Although Miranda was well aware that fraternal twins were no more alike than any other siblings, it seemed unusual to find a pair who were such total opposites. However, they got along well with each other, according to Irene, so perhaps their differences worked to their mutual advantage. "Enough wool gathering, Miranda" she said to herself and began to prepare the fish.

The work went smoothly and Miranda and her crew just had time to eat a hurried bite of supper in the cafe kitchen before the dinner traffic began. Miranda greeted her patrons at the front door and chatted with each group as she showed them to a table. For many of them, dinner at Miranda's along with her story hour had become a time-honored custom. Hawaiian vacations or the birth of a child or grandchild would occasionally mean missing a Saturday evening or two, but Miranda's "regulars" would leave word with a neighbor to tell Miranda so she wouldn't worry.

When all the diners had been served, Miranda stepped out into the cafe's herb garden. As she stood there quietly, she looked around her. The moon was just a sliver now and clouds moved over the glowing sickle from time to time. When the moon was hidden, the edges of the cloud covering her face seemed to light up. It was as if she was reassuring those who looked for her that she was still there even if they could not see her. Miranda dropped her hands to her sides and relaxed her body. She took three deep breaths. She became aware of a dark figure that seemed to be waiting for her at the end of the path. As the moon slipped silently behind a cloud, the softened light seemed to make the figure grow more solid.

"Hecate," called Miranda softly, "Is it you who will help me tonight?" The crone nodded mutely. "I am grateful, grandmother of the world, that your wisdom and your humor will enrich my story."

Again the figure nodded and, as she moved closer to Miranda, her twinkling eyes in their nest of wrinkles and her wry old lady's smile became visible. "Go, my child," she whispered in her paper-dry voice, "and know that we are with you."

Arlene Spector

As Miranda turned to go back into the kitchen, she had the feeling that someone had been watching her. She shrugged.

"It doesn't matter," she thought, "I'm the only one here who can see Hecate or hear The Goddess when she speaks to me"

*   *   *   *   *   *   *   *   *

When dessert had been served and coffee poured, Miranda stepped to the front of the large stone fireplace on the back wall of the dining room, and took her accustomed place on the high stool she always sat on to tell stories.

"Good evening, friends," she began. There was a murmur of return greetings from the crowd and then silence as they settled down and waited expectantly for Miranda's story for this evening.

"Tonight is a special night for our town," she began. "Dos Hermanas is celebrating her one hundred and fiftieth birthday today. In 1848, on this very date, Consuelo and Corazon Salazar, the two sisters after whom our town is named, first opened the doors of their hostelry just a few yards from where we are sitting now."

Some of the old timers among the audience smiled appreciatively. They knew that every year at about this time, Miranda would tell the story of the founding of Dos Hermanas—'Two Sisters,' in English. They also knew that every story was different from any of the previous tales. In fact, no one really knew how the town got its name. The records had been lost many years ago when the town had suffered a disastrous fire, after an earthquake, which almost totally destroyed every wooden building then in existence.

Miranda's Muse

"Few people remember these ladies any more, so this evening I shall tell you the unusual story of how it was that these two daughters of an aristocratic old Spanish family came to settle here in the California gold rush country."

As Miranda warmed to her subject, the room grew silent. Cups no longer clinked against their saucers, forks were laid to rest on dessert plates, and her listeners leaned forward expectantly. Last year, Miranda had told about the two sister having been "ladies of the evening," so they couldn't wait to hear what she had conjured up for them this year. She did not disappoint them. As her story unfolded, they were surprised all over again to discover the "new facts unearthed by a team of visiting historians from the University of Sacramento…" Miranda paused dramatically and then dropped her voice and began her story:

"In the beautiful city of Cordoba in Spain, there lived a wealthy and aristocratic family by the name of Salazar. Don Jose was the master of the house and head of the family. He was deeply concerned that the proud name of 'Salazar' continue for this and many more generations. Therefore, he was delighted to hear that the young wife of his eldest son was with child. 'Soon, the noble line of Salazar will have its heir apparent," he announced proudly, and gave orders that Dona Maria, the expectant mother of the heir, lack for nothing. Her every appetite and her slightest whim were to be fulfilled, and the local midwife, Señora Ernestina Lopez, was alerted and made it her business to call on the young woman each week to be sure that the pregnancy was going well.

"Then, one day during her third month of pregnancy the first flutter of apparent life was felt by Dona Maria. Her beautiful blue eyes grew wide as she sensed the movement of the child within her womb. 'My baby is wiggling within me,' she announced proudly. There was great happiness within the Salazar household. 'Our baby is already moving within his mother. This is surely a good sign of a healthy and active little boy!' the grandfather, Don Jose exclaimed.

"However, joy rapidly turned to dismay for poor Dona Maria. The kicking and thrashing of the babe within her womb became so strong that the poor woman could get no rest. Señora Ernestina tried everything she could think of to pacify the child, from a tisane of fragrant herbs to a gentle massage of the mother's belly, but nothing seemed to help. Finally, in desperation, three wise physicians were summoned to the Salazar castle.

"After examining the young mother carefully and then listening with their ears pressed firmly against Dona Maria's swelling abdomen, they conferred. Stroking their long gray beards and nodding wisely, they spoke: 'Dona Maria is carrying not one babe, but two little ones, praise God.'

"'But why,' wept the weary mother-to-be, 'Why do they thrash around so violently that I cannot sleep and can barely manage to retain my food?'

"'In our very wise opinions,' replied the physicians, 'they are fighting with each other, probably because they feel crowded. This is surely an indication of two large and strong little boys.' Again, the whole family Salazar buzzed excitedly at this news. 'Big boy babies! And two of them! We are truly blessed.'

"'But how can we persuade them to be still and let their poor mother sleep and eat?' wailed the poor lady.

"Again the three wise physicians conferred amongst themselves. 'Perhaps if we play soft music, they may rest more easily,' they suggested. Musicians were summoned and instructed to play lullabies and other soft, restful melodies. Pretty soon, everyone in earshot began to yawn and feel the need to doze, that is, all but the twins, for whom the music was intended. They thrashed and kicked even more strongly, so the musicians began playing hymns, hoping that the sacred music of the church might soothe the little ones. But to no avail. They kicked harder than ever. Finally, the musicians packed up their instruments and left, much more quietly than when they came. 'What you need is a priest,' they announced on their way out.

"So, a servant was sent to fetch Father Ignacio, the local priest, a very holy man indeed, known throughout Spain for his piety and humility. When he arrived, and saw the poor lady, he immediately fell to his knees and prayed mightily and loudly for guidance from all the saints in heaven, as well as the Trinity, individually and as a group. He remained on his knees for a day and a night. Finally, he rose unsteadily to his feet. 'These babies are possessed by demons,' he thundered. All drew their breath in sharply and cried out 'Demons! They are possessed by demons! How terrible! How awful! What must we do?' 'They must be exorcised,' Father Ignacio told them, 'and I shall begin immediately after I have eaten and slept, for it requires great strength to exorcise demons.'

"After he had eaten and slept, Father Ignacio summoned his acolytes and instructed them to bring incense and two large golden crosses. Finally, he was ready to begin. The incense burned day and night, releasing its heavy fragrance where the mother could smell the aroma of herbs and spices specially chosen for this purpose. The Holy Father and his aides prayed loudly and chanted the prescribed prayers and chants for exorcising demons, sprinkling gallons of holy water on all and sundry, especially Dona Maria. Finally, she fell asleep from pure exhaustion; still the little ones could be seen pushing and churning within their mother's body. So Father Ignacio gave up and left the Salazar household, and Dona Maria, that unfortunate lady, was left to sleep the sleep of one who had been through the tortures of Hell, or an exorcism, these things having much in common, or so it was said.

"Eventually, after many long and miserable months, Dona Maria's time came and she was brought to her childbed. Everyone in the Salazar household, from Don Jose himself down to the humblest stable boy waited anxiously to find out what strange unholy creatures might emerge. Señora Ernestina worked mightily to coax these babies forth, but they did not seem to want to oblige her. After thinking about it, she concluded that they each wanted to be the first born, and therefore neither would give way to the other. So, being a very wise and experienced midwife, she bent down very close to the laboring mother's abdomen and called softly to the twins: 'Little ones, do not fight. Your dear Mama wants to meet you. Come out now and I promise on my oath as a midwife never to tell anyone which of you came first.' That seemed to persuade the babies, and Señora Ernestina could see the top of a curly head and a pair of dainty feet emerging from their mother's body. When they were finally out in the world, it became obvious that they had contrived somehow to be born simultaneously, in a head to foot position. 'Never, in all my years as a midwife, have I seen such a birth!' the weary midwife exclaimed. When she had cleaned the little ones up and wrapped them in their swaddling clothes, Señora

Ernestina brought them to their grandfather, and announced: 'Don Jose, congratulations, you have two beautiful little grand-daughters, Praise the Lord!'

"At first, Don Jose was sadly disappointed, as he had set his mind on a grandson to carry on the family name, but when he laid eyes on the two beautiful little girls, with their silky black ringlets and their big blue eyes, he could not help but smile. Then, as he looked more closely, he began to laugh heartily. Each little face had one blackened eye and each had one bruised fist. 'Well, girls they may be, he laughed,' but they have the spirit of heroes, and no one will ever get the best of either one!' He shook his head in disbelief and ordered a celebration in honor of Dona Maria and her identical twin daughters, Consuelo and Corazon.

"Of course, it was assumed that when the two babies had all the space they needed in this great wide world, they would settle down and enjoy the cosseting they received from their doting parents, their wet nurses, their dry nurses, and the whole family Salazar - most especially their proud grandpapa. However, these two sisters, who were so identical in every way that not even their Mama could tell them apart, seemed to have carried their antipathy to one another in the womb along with them into their everyday lives. If Consuelo and Corazon were placed next to each other, both infants would scream and thrash about until someone ran to separate them. If by chance, they found themselves within arm's reach, they would grab fistfuls of each other's hair and poke at each other's eyes and nose most alarmingly.

"Finally, it was decided that they should be raised apart as much as possible for their safety and the peace and quiet of the Salazar family. Their cradles were placed in opposite corners of the nursery and each was assigned her own nursemaid and governess. At long last, there was harmony in the Salazar household once more, unless, by some mistake the twins were allowed contact with each other.

"As time went on, the little girls grew into beautiful young ladies with manes of black silken curls and eyes so blue, they were almost indigo. Still, the animosity between them flourished. When asked why they continued to trade insults and occasional blows with each other, neither one could say what had started it, or why she felt so hostile toward her twin sister.

"When they reached their fifteenth birthday, Don Jose began to make discrete inquiries concerning potential marriage partners among the aristocratic families of Spain for his beautiful and accomplished granddaughters. When the news got around that not only were they beautiful and well educated, but also that their wealthy grandfather had arranged generous dowries for them, Corazon and Consuelo did not lack for suitors.

"By this time, Don Jose had been assured of the continuation of the name of Salazar by the birth of a dozen or more boys to his sons and their fertile wives.

"Eventually, Corazon and Consuelo had chosen among the acceptable suitors their grandfather had pre-approved. The two young men, scions of noble families, were summoned to a private conference with Don Jose, along with their parents.

"'Gentlemen', began Don Jose, 'and Ladies,' he bowed to the two mothers-in-law to be, 'it is time to discuss the details of the matrimonial agreements I have arranged for my beloved granddaughters, Consuelo and Corazon. As you already are aware, I have settled a handsome dowry upon each of my granddaughters. They smiled and nodded. 'However, there is one condition upon which my final agreement to their marriages will be based.' The young men smiled, somewhat uneasily, while their parents sent worried glances back and forth across Don Jose's study. What could he possibly mean? Finally, one of the fathers-in law to be spoke up: 'And what is that condition, pray tell, Don Jose?' Don Jose took some time before he answered. After all, these were serious matters and not to be dealt with hastily. Finally, when the silence had become almost unbearable, he spoke: 'It is this,' he answered. 'Immediately after the two marriages take place, it shall be agreed that the two young couples make their new homes as far away from one another as is geographically possible.' After a moment or two, while the two families considered Don Jose's condition, they all broke out in happy smiles. The young men were so besotted with their fiancées that they would have agreed to almost anything and their parents were so delighted with the size of their dowries and the prospect of a connection with the noble Salazar family that they too thought this condition entirely acceptable. On the spot, they selected a date for the two couples to be married, or rather two dates, since Don Jose did not wish to risk fisticuffs or any other unpleasantness if the two brides were to share the same altar.

"After her wedding, Consuelo and her young husband boarded a clipper ship which took them to a lovely place in the Caribbean, where they took over the management of the Salazar sugar plantation on the infamous island of Santo Domingo. Of course the young couple did not think of it in these terms, since the event which made it so had not yet happened.

"Meanwhile, Corazon and her husband sailed on the same day, but on a different ship, to the beautiful city of San Francisco for their honeymoon, after which they would settle in Sacramento, California to manage the family's lumber and mining interests.

"Alas, after a short period of marital bliss, things began to go awry for the twins and their spouses. There was a massive slave insurrection on the Island of Santo Domingo and Consuelo's husband ended his poor young life prematurely by being thrown into the Caribbean by the rebellious slaves, where he drowned, being unable to swim, and was promptly eaten by a passing local shark. Consuelo escaped with her life and little else but the clothes on her back. She managed to stow away on a supply boat and when it dropped anchor at Galveston, in the great state of Texas, revealed herself and was immediately put ashore. Being a resourceful young woman and an excellent cook, she found employment at a local establishment. When she had saved enough money, she decided to make her way to the newly discovered California gold fields to see if she could make her fortune there. Being a Salazar and very proud, it never occurred to her to go home; her pride forbade such an ignominious retreat Instead, she decided to open a small hotel which she named "The Casa Don Jose", after her beloved grandfather.

"In the meantime, Corazon and her husband settled down in Sacramento and began to manage the family holdings. Her husband, however, had no experience with such things and proved his ineptitude by running through a large fortune in record time, leaving the noble family Salazar with nothing in the new world but debts. The young profligate was so mortified by his failure that he ran away with a red-haired dance hall hostess and was never heard from again.

"Corazon, realizing that she was now penniless, found a position as governess to the children of a wealthy railroad tycoon, who was impressed with her fine breeding and impeccable manners and hoped that some of it would rub off on his unruly children. Corazon did her best to teach her young charges manners and proper deportment. Her employer was pleased by her efforts and rewarded her with a generous bonus each year at Christmas. When she had saved enough, she left her position and traveled north to the California gold country, where she decided to open an inn in a small village outside of Ft. Bragg. She named it 'Villa Maria' after her blessed mother in Spain.

"Now neither sister knew of the other's presence, yet. Consuelo's Inn was on the west side of town and Corazon had built hers on the east side of town, facing the green and rolling hills. Their clientele were mostly gold miners who had found gold in 'them thar hills,' as they were fond of saying, and wanted to taste some of the refinements of civilized life with their newly made fortunes. They tended to be a rough lot, who needed to be taught some manners, which their stern and authoritative hostesses had no trouble in doing. The miners were only too glad to oblige them, since the food and accommodations were better than they had ever before experienced.

"After a while, the little town became famous for the two hostelries within its borders. So much so, that officers from Fort Bragg would ride there when they were not on duty just to partake of the hospitality and to bask in the company of their beautiful hostesses. By now, the two inns had lost their given names, being called 'Connie's Place' and

'Cora's Place' by the locals. Opinions were sharply divided as to which Inn was the better one.

Word began to make its way across town of another establishment across town run by a foreign lady who resembled her competitor most strikingly. Of course the sisters knew by now, that the other innkeeper was none other than her twin and nemesis. Needless to say, this did not sit well with either of them.

"Immediately, each young woman decided to do all she could to put the other out of business. Consuelo began to prepare the most wondrous gastronomic delicacies she could think of. The rich and spicy ragouts she prepared sent their mouthwatering aromas all over town and beyond. Fresh baked breads and the freshest vegetables prepared with olive oil and garlic brought hungry people from miles around to Consuelo's hotel. They were not disappointed. Delicate pasties filled with the freshest fruits and nuts almost floated, they were so light, and large cups of fresh ground and freshly brewed coffee left them fully satisfied.

When Corazon heard this, she redoubled her efforts in that direction, even to sending over to Fort Bragg for the freshest oysters and clams, and the finest fish brought in by local fishermen. She purchased a flock of chickens so that her roasted chicken with herbs and white wine would be the freshest and best tasting anywhere. Soon, the locals could be heard lauding Cora's efforts and swearing that they had never tasted such wonderful cuisine.

"When Connie heard of her sister's triumph, she redoubled her efforts. Along with the wonderful cuisine and hospitality she began to offer entertainment. Connie was an accomplished musician and had a beautiful contralto voice.

Soon, her guests were enthralled by her playing the guitar and singing the beautiful ballads of her native country.

"Naturally, word began to filter back across town of this new development. In response Cora hired a local musician to play for her. After a while she introduced her clientele to the art of flamenco dancing. And, to make matters worse for Connie, Cora cut her prices. Again, the fickle patrons came back across town to avail themselves of the bargain. When Connie was told of this situation, she cut her prices even lower than her sister's. Traffic across town reversed once more and it was not long before the price war between the two establishments had attracted all kinds of people from other places.

Hence, the town began to grow and as it did, the name of 'Dos Hermanas' or 'Two Sisters' came into common usage and stuck. Pretty soon everyone had forgotten the previous name of the little village, or even whether it had ever had another name.

"By this time, however, it became clear that the two warring twins could not keep running their inns at a loss, and if something didn't happen to stop it, they would both go out of business. The townspeople, delighted with the impact the two hotels had upon their town, realized this fact and were seriously concerned that their little town would once again become nothing more than a dusty outpost of the gold fields.

"So, a town meeting was called and all the citizens assembled in the town square, which was the only place which could accommodate the crowd. The two sisters were not there, as they were busy running their establishments into the ground. The meeting was called to order by the Mayor, who had been elected especially for this occasion, the town never needing much of a government before. The town folk grew silent while he outlined the problem. Then, talk went back and forth, forth and back as to what to do to stop the 'war of the two sisters,' as it was now called.

"Finally, Father Diego, the priest of the local mission, rose and held up his hands for silence. The crowd accorded him the dignity of his position and was still.

"'It seems to me,' he began, 'that there is a simple answer to our predicament. We must persuade the sisters to stop fighting and to get along with one another.'

"'Yes, yes,' agreed the Mayor, 'but how do we do that? They seem hell-bent for destruction, if you'll pardon my language, Father.'

"'We must persuade them that it is in their own best interests to do so,' replied the priest. 'I have a plan.' The townsfolk began to murmur among themselves. 'What kind of plan? What could he possibly mean?' Again Father Diego raised his hands for silence, 'If you will listen, I will explain.' And so they did.

"Let us offer these two accomplished young women a parcel of land in the center of our town. There is such a parcel, owned by the church, which I am sure I can persuade my superiors to sell to us for a very reasonable price. If we all contribute what we can afford, I am sure we can come up with the money. However, our gift of this parcel to the ladies under discussion will be conditional. They must agree to join forces and open one new hostelry, combining Cora's Place and Connie's Place into one establishment, to be named 'The Two Sisters,' or better yet, 'Dos Hermanas' as our town has come to be known. Further, they must forge a new sisterly relationship, so that this town can not only thrive, but that we can all live in peace and harmony as the good Lord has commanded.'

"And so it came to pass that Consuelo and Corazon agreed to close the Casa Don Jose and the Villa Maria and open a new larger inn called 'Dos Hermanas.'

"The twins had not seen each other for several years. Finally, when they stood face to face, each of them stared long and hard at the other. Unbelievably, despite the difficult times they had each encountered, they were as beautiful as ever. Finally, Corazon spoke, "Well, here we are." Consuelo agreed, "Yes, we are most certainly here." Then they stood quite still and thought. Finally, Consuelo asked her sister, "Why do we hate each other so much?" Corazon shrugged. "I have no idea…I suppose we must try to get along, if we are to be in business together." Consuelo nodded her agreement and said, "Yes, that is so," and they shook hands to seal the bargain.

"At first the twins treated each other with a chilly formality, but it did not take too long before they began to realize how advantageous it was to have a partner with whom to share the work, the problems and finally, the profits of their enterprise. Along the way, they found joy in sharing good times and bad with an equal. A genuine affection arose between Cora and Connie, and it was not unusual for them to hug and kiss to express their fondness for each other. Father Diego always stood ready to help settle a sisterly dispute, but even that became unnecessary as they got to know and love each other, as sisters should.

"And that, dear friends, is the true story of how 'Dos Hermanas got its name. And if others choose to believe that scurrilous rumor that got started last year, concerning the origin of our town, well, shame on them!"

Her audience burst into delighted laughter, knowing that Miranda herself had made up the "scurrilous rumor" herself last year.

"Goodnight, dear friends. Please stay and visit for a while and have another cup of coffee and some of Ruthie's special chocolate chip cookies on the house."

Closing time on Saturday nights was midnight and the doors were locked at eleven thirty. After the last patron had said "Goodnight," Miranda went into the kitchen, which was already cleaned up except for a few coffee cups still to be placed in the dishwasher. She thanked Ruthie, Dan and Mel for having worked so quickly and quietly. "I didn't hear so much as one 'clink' in the dining room," Miranda exclaimed.

As they all gathered up their coats and prepared to leave, Danny handed Miranda a manila folder. "Miranda, here's the first draft of the marketing plan I put together. After you and the professor have had a chance to read it over, I'd like to sit down with you to answer any questions or make any changes."

"That's fine, Danny," Miranda responded. "How about Monday?" This year Miranda had decided to close the cafe on Mondays, since it was usually a slow day, except during tourist season "Okay, I'll call before I come." Danny and Mel left. Miranda waited for Ruthie to put on her coat and was ready to go. "Goodnight, Miranda,' she said, and Miranda responded as always: "Goodnight, Ruthie and thank you for all your hard work."

As Ruthie drove off, and before she got into her pick-up, Miranda turned toward the garden and whispered softly, "Thank you, Hecate dear."

CHAPTER THREE

There is an old Jewish legend, which tells of thirty-six wise and holy people in each generation called "Zaddikim." No one knows who they are, but for their sake alone God allows the world to continue. Were it not for them, another catastrophe would surely envelop our Earth as the great flood did in Noah's time.

Sometimes it seemed as though Miranda might be one of the Zaddikim; so wise and thoughtful were her decisions. Take, for example, the first annual Dos Hermanas short story contest…

The Storysmith

*　　*　　*　　*　　*　　*　　*　　*　　*

Danny called Miranda at three thirty sharp on the following Monday. "Hi, Miranda, I've got the first rough draft of the marketing plan ready for you. When may I come over?"

"How about right now, Danny?" she replied, and went to remind Joseph that she needed his help assessing Danny's proposal. "Clearly, as a Professor of Business Administration, you are much better suited to seeing the positive and negative points to his plan than a poor ignorant working woman, namely yours truly."

"Why do I get the feeling that I am being set up for something?" asked Joseph plaintively, rolling his blue eyes toward the ceiling in mock chagrin.

"Perhaps, my darling, it's because you are - being set up, I mean." replied Miranda sweetly, with the wide eyes and fatuous smile of a Cheshire cat. She kissed him loudly and enthusiastically on the lips and then leaned back, with her hands still resting on his shoulders. "You will go over it with him, won't you?"

"Of course," he answered, "and when we're through working on it, we'll present you with the reworked copy. Okay?" Just then the doorbell rang, and Joseph went to let Danny in. Miranda waited a minute or two to greet him, and then the two men left the kitchen and retired to Joseph's office, chatting amiably about the latest news on campus. Miranda headed for the door into the garage.

"This is a perfect gardening day!" she decided. She took the gardening basket, where she kept all her hand tools—spades, pruning shears, and garden gloves—from the shelf, popped her beat-up old straw hat onto her head and stepped outside. She knelt and began to pull weeds, remove dead flowers from their stems and use the small hand cultivator to loosen the soil. It didn't take long before she pulled the garden gloves off and continued working with bare hands. She knew she'd surely have longer nails and softer hands if she kept the gloves on, but she loved the feeling of the cool moist earth between her fingers. She felt closer to her flowers and herbs as she gently pressed the soil around the base of each plant. It was like tucking the children into their beds; each one received her full attention before she left it and went on to the next.

She remembered when her children were little. Bedtimes were a special time for Miranda, as well as for her three little ones. It was a ritual that almost never varied. Just after they were bathed and cuddled dry in large fluffy bath towels, Miranda would lead the way to their bedrooms and begin the familiar sequence of events.

"What color pajamas would you like, the red ones or the blue ones?"

Each child would state his or her preference. After they were dressed in the color of their choice, they would put on their slippers and proceed to the kitchen table, where they were once again offered a choice.

"What would you like for your bedtime snack, a banana or cookies and milk?"

Once again, after serious consideration, each would announce which snack they would prefer. Miranda would comply with their wishes and they would chat quietly until they had finished. Then, all three would march to the bathroom to brush their teeth.

Finally, Miranda or Joseph would accompany them to their beds, where each night a different child would select the bedtime story. After it was read, everyone was tucked in and hugged and kissed. Miranda remembered the feel of their soft cheeks against hers, and their sweet clean scent as she nuzzled them just before saying: "Pleasant dreams and nighty-night. See you in the morning light."

They didn't notice that she never gave them a choice as to whether or when they wished to go to bed. Now and then, one of them would say: "I'm not sleepy yet, Mommy."

Miranda would reply, "That's okay. I'll leave your little lamp on for a while, and you may read to your Teddy or listen to the music box." It was never more than five minutes before she could return to the sleeping child and turn off the light. How she missed those long ago days! They had passed too quickly, and now her children were all grown up and lived far away from her. She let out a deep sigh and shook her head.

"If a parent does a good job of raising children, they become independent beings, capable of running their own lives and they move away and you miss them. Somehow, it doesn't seem fair...Well, who ever promised you 'fair,' Miranda?" she thought sadly, and planted another marigold seedling.

The afternoon flew by so quickly that Miranda was startled from her reverie when Joseph and Danny came out into the garden to find her. She gathered up her gardening tools, brushed off the knees of her jeans and headed for the garage. She replaced the gardening basket on the shelf and slipped off her dirty sneakers before going into the house.

Joseph and Danny had put out cups and saucers and cake forks, and put the kettle on to boil for tea. Miranda uncovered an apple cake she'd baked, and cut three generous slices. After they were all settled at the kitchen table, and enjoying their tea and cake, they began to talk about Danny's marketing plan for the cafe.

"Dan and I have gone over the outline of his plan and it seems to me to be do-able, so why don't you explain it to Miranda, Dan."

"Okay, Professor. First of all, Miranda, I think your contest idea is great! It could be a real winner if we work it out the right way. Time-wise, we should take about a month after we decide what the contest rules are, who the judges are and all that, to do the publicity campaign. In my opinion, we should limit the contest to people who live here in Dos Hermanas...at least for this first contest."

Miranda was astonished, "Just how many contests are you planning, Danny?"

"I don't mean to overwhelm you, but if the first one works out as well as I think it could, you may decide to make it an annual event."

Miranda thought about the idea for a few seconds, "Well, I'd like to reserve judgment on that until after we've tried it once. Joseph, you always tell me that everything always works perfectly on the blueprints, don't you?"

"Hoist by my own petard," he laughed, "and it's kept me from making a lot of mistakes."

Danny's enthusiasm was not dampened in the slightest by Miranda and Joseph's caution. "Now, it's important to work out the rules so everyone is real clear about them from the beginning. I put together my proposal for a list of rules that I think will keep things under control. First, as I said before, the contest should be limited to residents of Dos Hermanas. Anyone of high school age or more should be allowed to enter. That way, the creative writing classes at the high school can also participate."

"Interesting idea," said Miranda. "I didn't think of that, but I bet we've got a few budding authors at DH High and their teachers would probably be pleased to encourage their students to enter."

"Not to mention some of the teachers themselves," concurred Joseph.

"To continue, each entrant would be allowed to submit one unpublished story. When we receive the written copies, we remove the top sheet with the author's name on it, and assign the manuscript a number, so that no one but us can find out who wrote which story."

"That makes good sense," said Joseph. "It will reassure every one that the judging will be unbiased."

"After we get all the submissions, we give them to a panel of judges. It's important to pick people that everyone will trust to be fair."

"How about the local clergy?" suggested Joseph. "We could ask Father Dimitri at Saint Sophia's, and Reverend Wilson at the First Methodist Church."

"Sounds right, and to keep it ecumenical, I could ask Rabbi Moseson from the Fort Bragg Jewish Center," offered Danny.

"They certainly should be above reproach, but how about getting a few people from other occupations? Like English teachers. Your Mother teaches freshman English 101 at the college. D'you think she'd agree to be a judge? Obviously, none of the cafe employees or their families would be allowed to enter," said Joseph. They all nodded their agreement.

"Oh, I think I could persuade Mom to do it. And if you ask Dean Johnston from the college, that'll make five judges altogether."

"That ought to be enough," said Miranda. "How would the judging work after each submission has its own I.D. number, Danny?"

"We should ask each judge read each story and rate it on a scale of, say…one to ten, ten being the highest. Then we average the ratings and pick the top four or five stories."

"How about prizes?" asked Miranda. "Do you think a special gourmet dinner for the first place winner would be enough?"

"Well, if you included his or her family, that would be great," said Danny.

Joseph chimed in, "We could also award dinner for two for the other finalists, and if you really want to up the ante a little, lunch or dinner for each of the other entrants. That would encourage people to take a chance and enter."

"Can we afford to give away that many meals?" asked Miranda.

"I think so," opined Joseph. If things go the way I think they might, this contest would bring in more than enough patrons to take care of the costs of running it. Tell Miranda the rest of your plan, Danny."

"Well, here's where we could create a lot of interest in town and bring more people to the cafe. What we do is invite the four or five front-runners to present their stories at the cafe, say, on a Sunday evening, and let the listeners vote for the one they like the best. We could plan for four or five Sundays at the cafe. We'd offer a fixed price dinner plus one of our finalists telling his or her story. It could be special dinner, reservations required, with everything from soup to nuts."

There was silence while the three of them thought over this proposal. Finally, Miranda broke the silence: "It'd be a lot of work and expense up front, but I think it might just work…If we passed around rating sheets after dinner and the story presentation, the audience could do that rating right away while the story is still fresh in their minds."

"Great! And if use the same one-to-ten scale that the official judges use, we could tally all the scores right after the last story's been read and 'Voilà!' The Winner of the First Annual Dos Hermanas Story Contest will be announced at the cafe!"

They thought about it in silence again for a few minutes. Finally Joseph spoke up: "If this contest works out the way we have planned, everyone with a friend or family member who enters the contest will want to be there to offer support.

Some people will come just because it's a pleasant way to spend a Sunday evening, without leaving town."

"Yes," said Miranda, "And with a fixed price dinner, the planning is easy because we only need to offer two entrees from which to choose and with reservations in advance, there's no waste. I can take advantage of seasonal bargains at the wholesale market and keep costs down with no loss of quality. I think we'd want to keep the cost of these dinners reasonable—not much higher than our every day prices, so that none of our regular patrons will find it a hardship to attend."

Joseph agreed, "You're right, Miranda...good will means everything, especially in a town like Dos Hermanas."

As they lingered over their tea and cake, Miranda was impressed with the speed at which her original idea seemed to be taking shape once she brought Danny into it. It amused her to think that her main reason for running this contest, finding a replacement for herself, was still a secret. She rose from the table and asked, "Anyone for more tea and cake?" Since no one wanted more, she began to clear the table. "We might as well pick the dates for each of the events now, because we need time to get the publicity out. I think November first would be an auspicious day for the first presentation. Then, we could schedule three or four subsequent Sundays, depending on how many finalists we have. If we start each dinner at five p.m. sharp, people would still be home in plenty of time to get to bed at a reasonable hour."

"Well, that doesn't give us a lot of time, but November first it is! I'll get right to work on the fliers and the ads for the DH Gazette." Danny rose and gathered his materials, slipped on his sweater and with a cheerful "See Ya!" he let himself out of the front door.

Miranda and Joseph finished straightening the kitchen. As they turned out the light and went toward the living room, Joseph asked, "What's so auspicious about November first?"

"Oh, it's a special day for the Goddess," she replied and Joseph smiled. "Oh, I get it. What Christians call 'All Saint's Day.'"

"Right again, my love! And what Wiccans call 'Sam Haen.'"

CHAPTER FOUR

We will never know who the very first storyteller might have been, or why she desired to communicate more than what was needed for survival. Our cousins, the great apes, as intelligent as they may be, do not tell each other stories. No, there is something about story telling that is inherently human. Perhaps it was a mother who conceived the idea of creating a simple tale to soothe a restless child to sleep; or it might have been a bold hunter, so proud of his prowess in the hunt, that he needed to boast of his courage and skill; or, like Scheherezade, one of our early ancestors might have used the story teller's art to save her own life.

The Storysmith

* * * * * * * * *

The news of the contest spread like butter on a hot griddle. Neighbor told neighbor until the "Dos Hermanas Town Crier" picked up the story, to the delight of the cafe crew. It was the most popular subject of discussion at Hank's Barbershop and Shoe Shine Emporium, as well as at Maria's Beauty Salon.

Rumor had it that several of the town's well known raconteurs were racking their brains to come up with stories which could be considered "original," that is, that had never been published, nor were they those old chestnuts that had been told so often and for such a long time that no one could remember who had created them in the first place.

Miranda's Muse

Meanwhile, back at the cafe, the staff had met informally and divided up the work to be done to make the contest and its concurrent events happen. Danny took over designing and distributing fliers. Melanie agreed to compose a press release that would announce the rules of the contest, including the deadline for those wishing to enter their stories. Ruthie and Miranda put their heads together to come up with four menus that would allow two choices of entree, plus appropriate appetizers, side dishes, beverages and desserts.

Joseph wrote letters inviting each of the judges to become part of the panel that would evaluate the entries and select the finalists who would be invited to read their stories at the cafe. It didn't take long before each of the judges called and expressed their pleasure in being so honored. Naturally, all of them accepted.

Mrs. Simmons, head librarian, volunteered to receive all the manuscripts and Xerox them, store the originals in the library safe and remove all identifying material on the copies. She assured Miranda that she was the only one who knew the combination to the safe, "so there will be no chance of 'hanky-panky.'" Miranda smiled and accepted her offer, although she secretly doubted that such extraordinary precautions were necessary. The prizes for winning were modest ones, not the sort of thing someone would be likely to disgrace himself or herself for. Mrs. Simmons agreed to send each of the judges all the anonymous copies of the entries. "Then, I'll invite all of the judges to a meeting at the library conference room to do the rating and then to select the four or five stories with the highest rating for presentation at the cafe. Of course, I shall swear them all to secrecy," she assured Miranda. "Good idea, Barbara!" Miranda agreed. She wondered what sort of oath one would administer to four clergymen and the dean of a university.

Miranda kept track of all the details to make sure that nothing was left undone. Finally, she was satisfied that they had thought of every eventuality and covered it. She had done well to enlist the support of the Goddess; things happened just the way they were supposed to, with none of the "glitches" common to this sort of undertaking.

By October the twenty-ninth, four finalists had been chosen and to the somewhat surprised delight of all, the reservation lists were entirely filled. Miranda breathed a big sigh. "Well," she said to her crew, "we've all done our best to see that this contest goes off without a hitch. The rest is in the hands of the gods and goddesses."

* * * * * * * * *

November first dawned bright and blue, with small cloud puffs herded quickly toward the horizon by a brisk autumn wind. Miranda and Ruthie bustled around the cafe, making the final preparations to accommodate tonight's overflow crowd. Danny and Melanie came early to help set tables.

Joseph was stationed at the front door to greet people and seat them.

Now they were finished setting up and Miranda took a few minutes to check, one more time that everything was perfect. As she looked around, she felt satisfied with the charm of the decor she had carefully planned for this evening. Some of the usual blue and white tablecloths were there, but Miranda had added red and yellow-checkered cloths as well, and had placed a lovely arrangement of flowers, leaves and berries on each table with a candle the same shade as the tablecloth.

The patrons began to arrive a few minutes before five. The cheerful noise of their chitchat hummed and buzzed around the cafe. Occasionally, a burst of hearty laughter would emanate from one table or another. Miranda smiled as she mentally identified each laugher just from the sound. That merry contralto outburst, for example, belonged to Lucille Lorman.

She remembered once again the funny way they had become friends: If it hadn't been for the women's movement of the early seventies, it might never have happened. Lucy and Miranda met at the local college in a class entitled "Growth Experiences for Women." Lucy was not the kind of woman Miranda had ever befriended before. She was a waitress in a diner over in Fort Bragg, and in Miranda's eyes, she looked "cheap." When Miranda thought about her judgmental attitude in those days, she shook her head. "How could I have been such a snob?" she wondered. "Lucy is one of the kindest, funniest people I know."

The class assignment was to write an autobiography. It was Lucy's turn to read what she had written and Miranda didn't expect much from her. She was astonished and impressed by the fine quality of Lucy's writing. Lucy had told a story of her life as a foster child, moved from one foster home to another, abused and mistreated at most. It was a heart-breaking tale, told without dramatizing and with a remarkable sense of humor. If anything, Lucy's understatement of the horror she and her sister had endured made it all seem more poignant.

Two little girls, eight and five years old had been locked in a converted chicken coup every night, and had only each other to cling to when thunder and lightning terrified them. How could people be so cruel? Miranda admired Lucy's strength of character to have come through all of it with her humor and her sense of self intact.

She thought at the time that she might like to have Lucy as her friend, but there was one problem…a trivial one to be sure, but nevertheless, there it was: Lucy's wig. It was a fashion wig of the sort that was a brief fad in the seventies, but this one was a doozy! It was bright red and long, and it had lost some hair so that there was a white "bald spot" right in front at the hairline. It was bizarre! Miranda couldn't take her eyes off that damned white spot. It drew her attention like a magnet draws iron filings.

Finally, one day, Miranda could stand it no more. As the group sat in a circle listening as Lucy talked about where she'd like to be in five year's time, Miranda waited until she was finished talking and, as in a trance, arose from her seat and went over to Lucy.

"Lucy," she said, "I've been dying to do this ever since the first day of class," and she picked up the wig between thumb and forefinger as if it were carrion, and dropped it in the wastebasket. The other women sat dumbfounded by Miranda's action. They froze in their places, except that their eyes were wide open and darting from Miranda to Lucy and back again, as they waited for Lucy's reaction.

Lucy's perfectly nice shiny brown hair was tightly pinned closed to her head, to accommodate the wig. Slowly, Lucy removed the pins and shook her hair loose. Then, she got to her feet, and slowly went over to Miranda and, with a serious demeanor, Lucy looked into Miranda's eyes for a long moment. No one else in the room dared breathe. Then Lucy burst into delighted laughter, and she and Miranda fell all over each other, laughing and hugging, until finally everyone joined in. The others admitted that they too had hated that wig and liked Lucy's own light brown hair better.

"And that," thought Miranda, "was the beginning of a very special friendship." She went over to Lucy's table. "Oh, Lucy. I'm so glad you could come. I've missed you."

Lucy responded, "I'll call you, Miranda. And we'll make a date for lunch."

"Mondays are my day off," replied Miranda.

Lucy nodded and repeated: "I'll call you," - and Miranda knew she would. That's how Lucy was.

At seven o'clock, Miranda stepped to the front of the fireplace and raised her hands for silence. Almost immediately, the chatter and small-talk were halted by loud "Shhh's." When it was quiet, Miranda spoke: "Good evening, friends and neighbors." There was a murmur of response and then silence. "By now, I hope everyone has had time to finish dinner. If you'd like another cup of coffee or tea, please feel to help yourself from the carafes on each table. Tonight is the first event of the Dos Hermanas short story contest." A small ripple of applause spread through the audience. "The response has been most gratifying," continued Miranda. "Fourteen stories were submitted. After careful consideration, our judges chose four finalists. They are ready to present their stories here at the cafe. The first presentation will be tonight, followed by three more on subsequent Sunday evenings. Ruth and I have carefully selected a fixed price menu for your dining pleasure for each of these events. Those who subscribe to all four will do the final rating on rating sheets, which we'll hand out after each story. Please do sign your name, which will not be revealed, but so that we can be sure that only subscribers have voted. The winners will be announced here at the cafe at a special award presentation on the Sunday following the last story at three o'clock in the afternoon. Coffee and pie will be served, on the house." A cheer went up at this piece of good news. Miranda smiled at the exuberance of the response, and continued:

"I am pleased to present Rebekkah Proudfoot, our first finalist," Miranda announced. "Rebekkah's story is entitled 'Ma-Ya's Tale.'" She then took her seat near the fireplace.

An attractive young woman rose and made her way through the maze of tables to the spot usually filled by Miranda on her story evenings. A tall stool and a microphone awaited her. A soft light had been trained on the stool from above, so that it would not shine in anyone's eyes. Rebekkah settled herself on the stool and raised the microphone a few inches. Then she moved slightly to the side, so that it would not cover her face.

Rebekkah's finely chiseled features gave one the sense that she was a strong person with definite preferences. Her complexion was the color of mustard-flower honey. Her shiny dark hair was plaited into one thick braid tied at the end with black ribbon. It hung down her back almost as far as her narrow waist and tiny tendrils of hair had escaped the braid and curled themselves around her face.

For this occasion, she had chosen to wear a long black challis dress, paisley printed in soft shades of rose, turquoise and gold. The gathered bodice outlined her slim waist and small breasts; the long slightly puffed out sleeves ended in soft frills, which fell over her strong long fingered hands. Black suede boots showed from under the hem of her dress. A beautiful silver squash blossom necklace and earrings completed her colorful costume.

Rebekkah tucked her feet into the bottom rung of the stool, looked out at her attentive audience and smiled. Instantly, her face glowed as if lit from within. The listeners couldn't help but smile back at her.

"My story," she began, "is very old. My grandmother, 'Ruby', told it to me. She told me that her grandmother had told it to her, and so forth, back through the history of our people. There are many such stories, never written down, but passed on from one generation to the next in this way, but the one I am about to tell you is the oldest one of all. It goes back to the time when the earth was still new, and our people had just begun to live a tribal existence. It was even before we had learned to construct teepees, and so we had to shelter ourselves in whatever caves we could find.

"An old woman lived in a small cave near the plains. All around her she could see younger people at their tasks: hunting, gathering berries and herbs for food, caring for the babies and little children and watching the horizon for enemies or wildfires.

"'Ma-Ya,' as she was called, sat with a round stone in front of her. With a thick, sharp, flint chisel, she was working on the soft stone. 'I shall hollow out this stone and make myself a bowl to hold water. Then I will be able to bring water back from the spring in the daytime and save the long walk at night when I am thirsty and it is hard to see my way in the dark.'

"As she worked, Ma-Ya let her mind wander back to the time when she was young and good to look upon. The young men would follow her shapely form all over the encampment and down to the stream. They would fight just to be able to walk next to her. She had been very choosy, however, and had waited until the man she had chosen showed an interest in her. Then, they had gone together to dwell in the small cave in the low hills on the edge of the plains.

"She had brought forth children, but only a few had survived their childhood. Those who did had grown to adulthood, found their own mates and bore children of their own, but Ma-Ya's dimming eyesight could no longer pick her grandchildren out from the other youngsters of the tribe. Some time ago, an enraged bison had killed Ma-Ya's man during a hunt. Since that time, she had chosen to live alone in her cave. As she thought about all that had come to pass in her lifetime, Ma-Ya sighed and worked a little faster at hollowing out her bowl.

"Suddenly, Ma-Ya heard shouts: 'Fire! Fire! The prairie burns! The flames run toward our camp! Hide! Into the caves! Fire god is angry again! Run and hide!'

"Ma-Ya rose stiffly from her task. As she made her way into the darkness at the back of the cave, she thought, 'My old bones ache and it is hard to move quickly. Soon it will be my time to leave the camp, no more to be seen by my people, and wander out into the prairie where the coyotes, wolves and vultures rule.

"'Already, I hear them whisper when we eat together. I know what they say…that this old woman eats, but can no longer hunt or gather food; that it is time for me to go. Of course, they are right, only…I don't want to go just yet.'

"Ma-Ya smiled to herself as she thought of how she greeted each dawn, thanking the spirits that she was still alive to see the colors of sunrise and hear the laughter of the children as they played outside her cave. She would go out to greet them and offer them tidbits she had saved for them to eat. The smallest children would climb into her lap and beg for stories. Their warm little arms would wrap around her wrinkled old neck and she would stroke their hair lightly, gently undoing the knotted strands and combing them with her fingers.

"But this had been a hard time for the tribe. There had been terrible storms, which had flooded some of the lower dwellings, and then the fire god had gone on a rampage. What could be done to appease the fire god's appetite for the flesh of her people? Ma-Ya crawled to the very back of her cave to wait out the firestorm. Soon, she fell asleep.

"When Ma-Ya awoke, she remembered she had dreamt. In her dream, the fire god had spoken to her. She sat cross-legged and thought about her dream. Finally, she decided what she must do.

"That evening, the people came cautiously out of their caves to see who had survived the fire god's wrath. One hunter and two children were unaccounted for. As the mate of the hunter fell to the ground, the mothers of the two children wept in each other's arms. Ma-Ya went to them and put her arms around their shoulders.

"'My sweet ones, I grieve for you and your children. I will pray to the gods that they may find comfort in each other in the afterlife, as you have found comfort in each other here'.

"Then she went to the dead hunter's woman and squatted next to her. The woman wept uncontrollably and thrashed about on the hard ground. Ma-Ya began stroking the woman's head and then her face, all the while making soothing sounds deep in her throat. Slowly the woman became quieter and then silent, and when Ma-Ya gathered her into her sinewy old arms, she fell into quiet weeping. As Ma-Ya rocked back and forth, she spoke words of comfort. 'My child, in time the pain will lessen and you will love again, but for now, it is good to weep out your sorrow.'

"Gradually, the young woman was able to catch her breath once more. Ma-Ya continued to hold her and began to breathe long slow breaths. The woman began to follow Ma-Ya's breathing pattern with her own, until she was very still. Her eyes closed and she slept. Gently, Ma-Ya lowered her to the earth and covered her with the fur robe she had put on when she left her cave.

"Then Ma-Ya stood and spoke to her people: 'It is clear that the fire god is angry. We must make a sacrifice to him.'

"O-Sa, the tribal leader, answered: 'We have already sacrificed a whole bison to the fire god. Still the fire comes and consumes our people.'

"Ma-Ya answered: 'Perhaps the fire god has no taste for bison. Evidently he hungers for the flesh of the people.'

"There was a loud murmur from the crowd. 'What does she mean? A human sacrifice?'"

"'I am an old woman,' continued Ma-Ya, 'and it is time for me to return to the earth mother. I offer myself as a sacrifice to the fire god, so that he will no longer take our young ones.' The people gasped and gazed at Ma-Ya in silence and great awe. She spoke: 'When the fire god comes again, I will walk out to meet him.'

"Several weeks passed and the watchers on the hilltops were quiet, as there were no storms or prairie fires to warn the people about. Every day, Ma-Ya climbed to the hilltop to look for herself. Then she returned to her cave to meditate and to make preparations for her sacrifice. She received frequent visitors. They came to be with her, and although they did not mention her sacrifice, it was clearly on their minds. When they left Ma-Ya, they said a tender farewell and touched her hands and face lovingly.

"On the morning of the next fire, Ma-Ya rose and looked out of the cave entrance. She could see dark clouds overhead and, as she came outside, a distant rumble of thunder sounded. She climbed to the hilltop and, as she and the young man assigned to the morning watch peered into the distance, they saw a spear of lightning flash through the sky and dart down into the grassy plain. A loud crack of thunder reached her ears and then she saw the plume of smoke rising from the dry grass. The young watcher saw it, too. He cupped his hands around his mouth and shouted: 'Fire! Fire in the prairie, coming this way!'

"Ma-Ya hurried to her cave to gather the things she would need for her sacrifice. She put on a robe of rabbit skins, which she had trapped, scraped and laboriously sewed together. Then she took a stout wooden staff that she used for her walking stick. She went to the very back of her cave, where it was coolest, and took a skinned rabbit carcass she had been saving for this occasion. She picked up the drinking bowl she had finished chiseling and wrapped it with soft dried grass from her sleeping place. She tied the rabbit and the bowl into the skin pouch she had fashioned of hide and looped the strap over one shoulder and diagonally across her chest. Then she settled the pouch so that it sat comfortably on her bony hip. As she did this, she remembered the many times she had carried her babies in just this way.

"Finally, Ma-Ya picked up a strong green tree branch with leaves and berries still clinging to it, which she had broken off a tree near the mouth of her cave. She stepped outside and brought the tree branch to an upright position. As she stepped carefully down the hill, she carried it like a banner. Despite their fear of the fire, her people had come to the path and were waiting silently on either side, leaving a clear path for Ma-Ya to begin her last walk out of camp.

As she turned toward the waiting prairie, everyone was silent. Then a small child called out to her, 'I love you, Ma-Ya.' Some began to weep because they would see their old friend no more. Ma-Ya said nothing, but she smiled and blessed them all silently.

"Ma-Ya walked very slowly, but steadily toward the fire. Since she had seen that first plume of smoke, the fire had increased in size and intensity and was burning rapidly across the prairie in front of her. She turned to her left and continued walking until she began to feel its heat on her face and body. The wind blew from the east and grew stronger as it drove the fire toward the west. Ma-Ya stopped for a few minutes when she reached the black stubble of grass that the fire god had already consumed. She took three deep breaths and calmed herself. As she let all fear melt from her body, she suddenly felt light as air and disconnected from her surroundings. She stepped out onto the still smoldering stubble and, although she was aware of the heat, it did not burn her. She reached into the pouch, brought out the rabbit carcass and impaled it on her branch. The branch arched down toward the scorched earth. Ma-Ya bounced it a few times to make sure it was secure. When she was satisfied, she took her walking stick and began to follow in the fire god's black footsteps. As she did, she began to chant.

"At first, her chant had no words, but then Ma-Ya began to sing, 'Oh, great and terrible fire god, please accept our sacrifice. We beg of you to tell us how we can best serve you.' She began to move more quickly toward the flames. The wind at her back seemed to push her forward. 'The fire god seems eager to consume my sacrifice,' she thought. As she steadied herself with her walking stick, Ma-Ya swung the branch with its cargo of skinned rabbit around in front of her. 'This old woman's flesh is tough and dry, oh great One,' she chanted. 'I bring with me this fat and juicy young rabbit. Eat it's flesh and mine, too, if you desire it.'

"Ma-Ya kept moving steadily forward, still holding the rabbit into the flames just ahead of her. The rabbit began to lose its reddish color. As it turned brown and it's juices began to drip into the fire, a delicious aroma rose into the air. Ma-Ya's mouth began to water. Nevertheless, she continued following the fire and holding the roasting carcass into the flames. The more quickly Ma-Ya went, the faster the flames seemed to move away from her. As she trekked stolidly forward, she noticed that the end of her walking stick, which she had been jamming into the edge of the firestorm to help pull herself forward, glowed red-hot and the rabbit was beginning to char.

"Ma-Ya began to slow down. She could not remember being as tired or out of breath as she felt now. Finally, she stopped. 'Well, then, fire god, what DO you want from me?' She held her breath and with closed eyes, waited to hear the fire god's answer.

"The people who had watched Ma-Ya leave on her fatal mission now peered into the distance to see if they could discern the figure of the old woman in the flames. One of the watchers on the hill, known for his keen eyesight, called down to them, 'Ma-Ya stands among the flames.' A low moan welled up from the crowd, 'Our beloved Ma-Ya; how frightened she must be!'

O-Sa, the chief, called out to them, 'Let us beseech the fire god to have mercy and not make Ma-Ya suffer long.' The people fell to their knees and prayed for Ma-Ya.

"Meanwhile, Ma-Ya stood quietly with her eyes closed. She could hear the crackling of the fire as it moved further and further to the west. For a moment, she did not know where she was, so deeply had she listened to the voice of the fire god. She opened her eyes slowly and looked about her. She could see the smoke from the fire as it rose toward the western sky. Dark clouds were gathering together; they rolled and tumbled about furiously and from their midst, Ma-Ya saw a dagger of lightning strike the plains again. A few second later, she heard the rumble of thunder as the clouds opened up and drenched the plains and the fire with dark water from the firmament.

"'Thank you, oh gracious one, for your mercy,' she prayed and sank slowly to the dark stubble at her feet. As she let go of the branch with the rabbit still attached and laid down her walking stick, she noticed that the tip still burned red. She smiled and thought, 'It seems the fire god has other plans for me.'

"She reached into her pouch and brought out the small stone bowl. Then she set it down in front of her and took some of the soft dry grass in which she had wrapped it. She pulled out a tuft and placed it in her bowl. Then she picked up her stick and knocked the red-hot tip against the rim of the bowl. It broke off and fell into the dry grass. As it flared up briefly, Ma-Ya gazed at it in wonder. As she watched the flame die down and begin to burn with a small steady flame, she fed it a few more bits of dry grass. Then she turned her attention to the rabbit carcass. As she pulled it off the branch, she scorched her fingers and quickly stuck them into her mouth to cool them. The meat juices were very tasty, so she tore off a bit of the flesh and ate it. It was succulent and savory, and she was tempted to eat more, but she placed it in her pouch instead. When she had rested, she rose and, leaning heavily on what was left of her walking stick, picked up her bowl with its precious contents and started back to camp.

"She turned southwest and trudged wearily toward the low hills. In her left hand, she cradled the small bowl with the tiny flame. Periodically, she would stop to catch her breath and to reach in to her pouch for bits of dried grass to feed the little flame and keep it burning. When the encampment was at last in sight, Ma-Ya paused once again. She pulled her shoulders back until she stood as tall as she was able. Then she began to walk slowly and majestically back into the center of camp. Her people stared at her as if she were an apparition. No one made a sound, but they shrank fearfully away from her.

"'Be not afraid, my children. I am no ghost. The fire god spared my life and sent me back to you with a message.' Then, she slowly sank to the ground, carefully placing the bowl of fire before her for all to see.

'What's that? ...What did the fire god say? ...What happened? ...Are you hurt, Ma-Ya?' All the questions seemed to burst forth at the same time. Ma-Ya wearily shook her head and raised one hand to stem the flow of chatter.

'Quiet, my children,' she whispered, 'I am weary beyond words. Let me rest first and then I will tell you everything.' Someone brought her water and they hushed each other loudly, making even more of an uproar than before. Finally, they settled down, gathered in a circle around Ma-Ya and waited for her to speak.

"Soon she was rested enough to begin. 'The fire god spoke to me. He does not wish us to hate him and fear him anymore. He wishes to dwell among us, helping us to know his ways, so that he may be loved and revered as he wishes. He gave me a wondrous gift to bring to you. You see it before you in this stone bowl. It is a flame from his great fire.

We are to build an altar so that the fire god may dwell safely among us for all time. A shallow pit must be dug in the very center of our camp. Stones shall be brought to make a ring around this pit. Then straw and dry wood shall be placed within the holy circle of stones. When that is done, this small flame that I carried to you shall be placed in the center of the circle so that it may continue to burn forever and grow larger in our midst.

"'When our hunters bring us game, we shall sacrifice it by holding it over the flames. When the sweet smell of the meat rises toward heaven, the fire god will be satisfied. When the flesh has turned brown, we are to honor the sacrifice by partaking of the meat. In these ways will we worship the god of fire.'

"With this, she reached into her pouch and brought forth the cooked rabbit carcass. She tore off a small piece and popped it into her mouth. As she chewed the delicious morsel, she took another small piece and handed it to O-Sa. He tasted it and smiled. Ma-Ya pulled off more bits of rabbit and passed them among the others until all had partaken. They smacked their lips and exclaimed that they had never eaten more delicious food. Ma-Ya smiled and nodded in agreement.

"'This fire must never be allowed to die,' she began again, 'In each generation, the fire god has chosen the oldest member of the tribe to be 'Keeper of the Flame.' When we move to another camp, this person will take some of our campfire and keep it alive in this stone bowl until the new altar is ready for it. Thus did the fire god command us.'

"Ma-Ya became the first 'Keeper of the Flame'. Her people honored her for her sacred duties, as well as her wisdom and courage in meeting the fire god face-to-face. Ma-Ya lived to be very ancient indeed, caring for the flame and instructing the young in the proper ways to use the fire god's gift. Ever since those long ago days, our tribe has continued to honor the oldest among us as 'Keepers of the Flame'. And that, dear friends is the end of my story."

The diners in Miranda's Cafe sat quietly for a moment and thought about Rebekkah's tale. Then, as Rebekkah climbed down from the stool, they applauded vigorously until she bowed to each side of her audience and rejoined her family at one of the tables.

CHAPTER FIVE

There is a Knowing beyond knowledge and a Sensing beyond the senses. Miranda was privy to this world beyond. It was not unusual for her to look up from the task at hand as though she had heard something. She would rise and walk toward the telephone. A few seconds after she got there, the phone would ring and Miranda would pick up the receiver and greet the caller by name, even before a word had been spoken. There were other manifestations of this ability as well...

The Storysmith.

*   *   *   *   *   *   *   *   *

On Tuesday morning, Miranda awoke from her early morning slumber with a start. She lay quietly beside Joseph, who was still snoring softly, and thought. She wondered why she felt so jumpy. Perhaps it was an upsetting dream that she couldn't remember. She sat up and carefully got out of bed, so as not to wake Joseph. As she slipped into her fleece robe, she continued to consider what might be bothering her. As she went through her mental catalogue of potential subjects for concern, she could find nothing important to worry about. She chuckled to herself, "My problem is that I have nothing to nail my anxiety to. What a silly state of affairs!"

She splashed her face with cold water and ran a brush quickly through her tangled hair. In the few minutes it took

Miranda's Muse

Miranda to do this, Joseph woke up and was already tying the belt of his brightly striped bathrobe. "G'morning," she greeted him and went to collect the first hug and kiss of the new day. Together, they headed for the kitchen where the coffee was already perking in the automatic coffee maker.

"Mmm, that sure smells good," said Joseph. "What did we ever do before Mr. Coffee?"

"We got up earlier," responded Miranda wryly.

Joseph poured them both a cup of the fragrant Kona blend they liked and added milk. After taking a sip of coffee, Joseph delivered his ritual morning weather report: "Looks like a clear, cool day today," he said, peering out of the window, When he turned away from the window, Miranda was already pouring orange juice. "Did you sleep well, my dear?"

"Well, yes, I slept very well, but I woke up feeling really nervous—practically jumped out of my skin. I've been trying to pin down what could be causing it, but I still haven't a clue." Miranda popped two bagels into the toaster and then opened the refrigerator to bring out the butter dish and jam pot.

"The last time you felt jumpy, we had an earthquake. I hope this isn't a predictor."

Miranda laughed, "I hardly think so, Joseph. Think of all the previous quakes we've had. I certainly didn't predict them!" Just then, the bagels popped up and right out of the toaster onto the tile counter.

"I don't think we should eat those bagels," quipped Joseph. "They're not dead yet." They sat down and buttered their bagels. The first crunchy, buttery bite was always the best and worthy of a few minutes of quiet munching and appreciating. Miranda broke the silence.

"Anything special happening today, Joseph?"

"Nothing much," he replied. "The usual—a meeting of the curriculum committee to finalize course offerings for the summer semester. Pretty standard stuff. That, and the case presentations in my 'Business Policy' course."

"What did you think of Rebekkah's story?" continued Miranda. "Do you suppose it is actually tribal folklore?"

Joseph paused in mid-chomp.

"It never occurred to me that it was anything else. What do you think?" he asked.

"From what I know of Rebekkah, she's certainly creative enough to have concocted the story. Ever since she wrote her Master's thesis on the folklore of her tribe, she's been considered an expert on the subject. She has a rich tradition to draw from, so my guess is that her story is mostly true, with a little embellishment here and there."

Joseph nodded. "Sounds logical to me."

Miranda finished her last bite of bagel. "It's time I got on my way," she said. See you later."

*   *   *   *   *   *   *   *   *

When Miranda pulled into the cafe's parking lot a little while later, she felt calmer.

"There's nothing like getting back into a familiar routine to chase the 'heeby-jeebies," she thought.

Ruthie's car was already there. As Miranda entered the back door, Ruthie was just hanging her sweater up. "G'mornin, Miranda. Everything okay?"

Miranda placed her jacket on the hook next to Ruthie's.

"Oh, I guess so. How was your day off?"

"It was busy, to be sure. We went to Fort Bragg shopping and I bought myself a real nice dress for Christmas and New Year's Eve."

Miranda shook her head.

"I keep forgetting how close the holidays are. Thanksgiving will be here before we know it," said Miranda.

"That's so," agreed Ruthie. "The holiday season begins earlier every year, it seems to me. The stores are already decorating for Christmas and it's not even Halloween yet. It won't surprise me if the tinsel and holly are up at the fourth of July next year."

The two women began to prepare for the day's business. Ruthie opened the dishwasher and began to stack the clean dishes on the counter. Miranda lit the gas griddle.

"While the griddle heats up, I'm going to check yesterday's mail, Ruthie."

Ruth nodded and went to fetch the stepladder so she could put the dishes away in the high cabinets.

Miranda pushed through the swinging doors into the cafe dining room. She could see a bunch of oddly assorted letters, magazines, shopper's guides and sale fliers lying beneath the mail slot in the front door. As she went to pick them up, she began to feel a little disoriented, as though the floor was moving under her feet. She grabbed the back of a chair, held on and closed her eyes. She heard a sound like waves rolling in from a stormy sea. It grew louder and closer to the cafe from the southwest.

"Oh my God," she muttered. "It's an earthquake!"

She moved quickly away from the windows and toward the closest table. Yanking a chair out, she dove under the table. Everything began to shake. The window shutters rattled like chattering teeth on a cold morning, and one of the decorative wall plates fell down and shattered into a million pieces.

"This feels like at least a five pointer," she said to herself in her refuge under the table.

At that moment she heard a loud crash and a scream and then breaking dishes.

"Oh, my God, Ruthie!"

She crept out of her hiding place and made for the kitchen. At first, she didn't see Ruthie. But as she moved quickly around the large worktable, her heart suddenly began to palpitate like a trip-hammer. She ran to where Ruthie lay with her head against a cabinet. The stepladder was on its side on the floor and there were broken dishes all around her. Her right leg was twisted beneath her at an awkward angle. Miranda knelt at her friend's side and took her wrist to check for a pulse.

"Thank God, she's still alive."

At the sound of Miranda's voice, Ruthie's eyes opened. She groaned and then tried to move, but Miranda held her still and cautioned her:

"Don't try to move, Ruthie. There's been an earthquake and you fell off the ladder. I'm going to call the first aid squad, so please hold as still as you can."

She waited a moment longer until she was sure that Ruthie was fully conscious. Then she picked up the phone and dialed the EMT number, which was written just above the telephone box. She knew the 911 lines would be swamped by this time.

"EMT - Dos Hermanas Station," answered a familiar voice.

"Charlie, this is Miranda at the cafe. There's been an accident. Ruthie fell off a ladder and I think her leg is broken. She must have hit her head against a cabinet when she went down. She was unconscious when I found her."

"We'll be right over, Miranda," answered Charlie and hung up.

Miranda returned to Ruthie's side.

"Don't move, Ruthie. Charlie and the team are on the way."

"Okay," whispered Ruthie and groaned. "My head hurts somethin' awful and I can't feel my right leg."

Miranda nodded, "I know Ruthie. Just lie still; I hear Charlie's siren already."

Miranda went to the linen cabinet and took out a large linen tablecloth. She shook it out and then covered Ruthie's inert form up to the neck. Then she knelt and held her friend's hand. A moment later, the ambulance pulled up at the back door. A young man and a woman rushed through the back door into the kitchen.

Miranda rose and got out of their way. Charlie examined Ruthie's leg gently and expertly, while Jan, the other technician took her vital signs. "Pulse is rapid and B.P. is a little high, but that's understandable under the circumstances. I'll keep watch that it doesn't go higher."

Charlie nodded and spoke up:

"The right leg is definitely broken, but I think it's a clean break. I'll get the splint and then we'll have to straighten it out before we try to move her."

He went outside momentarily and returned with a device that would immobilize the leg. Charlie knelt at Ruthie's side once more.

"Ruthie, we have to straighten your leg so we can get you onto a stretcher without doing any more damage. It's going to hurt, but we'll be quick about it, so it won't hurt for more than a few seconds. Can you handle a few seconds of agony?"

Ruthie smiled faintly. "You sure make it sound like fun, Charlie; how can I refuse? Okay, do your worst."

Charlie and Jan moved into position on either side of their patient.

"Miranda, you kneel by Ruth's head and hold her shoulders down."

Miranda complied quickly and braced herself against the cabinet while she held Ruthie's shoulders still.

"Okay, here we go," said Charlie.

As the leg was straightened, Ruthie drew her breath in sharply and bit down on her lower lip to stifle a scream.

"Yell if you want to," said Jan, but Charlie had already slid the open brace under Ruthie's leg and was closing the straps that held it in place.

"Well, that should do it," said Charlie. Jan checked Ruthie's vital signs again.

"Her pressure and pulse rate are starting to go down. I'll go get Gus and the stretcher. A few minutes later, a large muscular black man wheeled a stretcher into the kitchen. Gus and Charlie bent down and gently moved Ruthie onto the stretcher, which had been lowered to the floor. She groaned once and then closed her eyes.

"We'll check her for concussion," said Jan. She shook out a khaki colored wool blanket and covered Ruthie up.

Gus and Charlie raised the stretcher on its hydraulic lift and wheeled it and Ruthie outside and into the ambulance. As they pushed the stretcher into its slot in the back of the ambulance, the wheels of the stretcher automatically folded up. Jan climbed into the back with Ruthie, while Charlie rode in the passenger seat next to Gus. As the gleaming white ambulance pulled out of the driveway, the siren started wailing and hooting and the lights started flashing to warn traffic out of the way.

Miranda turned back into the cafe, and went inside to call Ruth's husband. After several tries, Miranda was finally able to reach him.

"Clyde, this is Miranda at the cafe. Ruthie fell off a ladder during the quake and broke her leg. She's on her way to the hospital right now by ambulance."

Clyde was silent for a moment while he took in what Miranda had just said. Then he responded, "Okay, Miranda, I'm on my way. I'll call you later."

"Thanks, Clyde. I'd appreciate that."

Miranda hung up the phone and noticed that her hands were shaking. She poured herself a glass of cold water and slowly drank it down. She said, to no one in particular,

"Okay. I give up."

As long as she could remember, Miranda always reacted to emergencies in this way. At first, she was like a piece of well-oiled machinery, taking charge and doing everything quickly and efficiently as though she hadn't a nerve in her body. Then, when she had taken care of everybody else, and the coast was clear, she fell apart. Right now, for example, she sat down on the floor and began to weep as though she would never stop. Then, like a summer squall, it was over. She breathed deeply to regain her composure, and then rose and went to wash her face.

At that moment, she heard a car pull up behind the back door and a moment later, Joseph rushed in, car keys still in his hand.

"Thank God you're okay," he said. "I've been trying to get through by phone, and when I couldn't, I jumped into the car and came right over."

Miranda went to him and they hugged one another and held onto each other for a long comforting moment. He took in the scene around him.

"Well it looks like we lost some crockery. Is everything else okay?"

"No, I'm afraid not," she replied. "Ruthie was on the step ladder putting things away when the quake hit. The ladder fell over with her on it. Her leg is broken, and she may have a concussion. I called the emergency squad and she's on her way to the hospital."

"Oh, poor Ruthie, that's terrible."

Joseph looked at the mess of broken pottery, went to the broom closet and started sweeping up the shards. Miranda went out into the dining room to see if any of her regulars had yet made it to the cafe. She unlocked the front door and let in her first customer of the day.

"Good morning, Mr. Taylor. I might have known that not even an earthquake could keep you from your morning cup of coffee."

"That little wiggle," he answered. "Why that hardly qualifies as a real quake, Miranda. Now the San Francisco quake back in '06 that was a quake worthy of the name!"

Miranda smiled.

"So I've heard. Were you there, Mr. T?"

He puffed out his chest and said proudly,

"I should say so! Of course I was just a little tike then—couldn't have been more than four or five at the time, but I sure haven't forgotten how scared I was—wet my pants, as I remember."

Miranda chuckled,

"Well I'm glad that this little temblor didn't scare you that much, Mr. Taylor…Now what can I get you? The usual?"

"I guess so. Orange juice, real coffee…not that unleaded stuff, and a bear claw, warmed up," he said, referring to a sticky nut-laden pastry he had a special fondness for.

"Oh, I'm sorry, but the bakery hasn't delivered this morning, yet. I imagine the traffic is snarled on account of the quake."

The old man made a face.

"Too bad, I was fancying one of those today. Well, how about some whole wheat toast with some of your home-made marmalade?"

"That, we can do," replied Miranda and headed back into the kitchen.

Joseph was just finishing dumping the broken pottery into the trash bin.

"Joseph, would you mind fixing Mr. Taylor's order? He'd like whole-wheat toast with butter and my marmalade, and regular coffee. I'm going to try to get through to Danny and Mel. I hope at least one of them is available to help out today."

She paused for a moment, "You didn't happen to hear a radio broadcast on your way in, did you, Joseph?"

"Yeah. They said it was a little over five points on the Richter scale. The epicenter is on the ocean floor to the southwest of us. They don't know yet if anyone else got hurt."

Miranda picked up the phone and was grateful to hear the dial tone once more. She made her call and waited impatiently for someone to answer. She drummed her fingers nervously on the table as the phone rang once, then twice and finally Irene Schoenberg's familiar voice greeted her.

"Good morning. Irene here."

"Irene, this is Miranda. I'm at the cafe; we've had an accident. Ruthie fell off a ladder during the quake and broke a leg."

"Ohmigod!" exclaimed Irene. "How can I help?"

"Joseph drove in and he's here waiting on customers. Are either of the twins available to work today?"

"Danny's here now and should be able to come in. The campus is closed until at least tomorrow, while they check for damage. Melanie spent the night at a friend's house so they could study together. I'll try and reach her there…Danny says he can come in and I'll come with him to help out," offered Irene.

"Oh Irene, are you sure? You must have a million things to do."

"Nonsense, Miranda. I'm an experienced cook and bottle washer. What kind of a friend would I be if I didn't help out in an emergency?"

"Well," said Miranda, "Since you put it that way, how can I refuse? Thanks a million!"

Miranda replaced the receiver back in its cradle and began to set up for the breakfast patrons.

"They're late coming in today, things being what they are, but I bet they'll be hungry, and eager to trade stories about 'Where were you when it hit?'" she told Joseph.

* * * * * * * * *

Later that day, Miranda hung up the phone and breathed a large sigh of relief.

"Irene, Joseph, Danny," she called, "That was Ruthie, calling from the hospital. She's going to be okay once her leg knits. The doctor said that he thinks she'll be on crutches for six weeks at the outside. Then, if her leg is knitting properly, she ought to be able to come back to work, at least part-time to begin with."

Just then, Melanie came through the back door.

"Hi, everyone," she said. "What's going on? I got Mom's note when I got home. She said Ruthie got hurt and I should come right over."

Miranda replied, "Thanks, Mel. We can use all the help we can get…I think the first thing we need to do is get organized. If each of you would make out a schedule of your availability, we could work out a system that would make some kind of sense."

She thought for a moment and then turned to Joseph.

"If it's okay with you, my dear, I'd like to keep you on call to fill in when necessary. I know you've got other important work to do, and I think we can manage without you, except for Saturday and Sunday evenings."

Joseph nodded and replied. "If you have enough help for today, I could use the time to catch up on a special project I've been working on."

Miranda nodded. "Okay. Then I'll see you this evening when I get home," she said, and saw Joseph to the door and kissed him goodbye.

As Miranda turned back into the cafe, Irene and the twins were already jotting their schedules down on some notepaper.

"Miranda," said Irene, "I've been thinking. If this accident had to happen, it sure picked a convenient time as far as my schedule is concerned. As it happens, this is the beginning of exam week. I can easily get my exams proctored by my teaching assistant. After that, we get into Thanksgiving vacation and then Christmas break. I won't have to be back on campus until after New Year's. So I can give you a lot of time. How about it, Miranda? Can you use a new assistant until Ruthie gets back?"

Miranda was overwhelmed by her friend's generosity.

"Are you sure you know what you're letting yourself in for, Irene? It can get pretty frantic around here, you know."

"I'd like to give it a try," said Irene simply.

"Well, in that case, and before you can change your mind, I accept your kind offer, but I insist on paying you the going rate for the work you do. You're too much of a hotshot in the kitchen for anything less. Now, are you sure your work at the college won't suffer? The last thing in the world I'd want to do is to cause you problems."

"Just to be certain, Miranda, I'll check it out with the Dean," offered Irene.

"Fair enough" agreed Miranda, "and thank you from the bottom of my heart." Irene came over to Miranda and the two friends hugged each other warmly.

CHAPTER SIX

Hearing a neighbor tell a story became more popular than television in Dos Hermanas! For those who, as children, had attended Barbara Simmon's Saturday Story Hours, it was only natural. When Mrs. Simmons opened the pages of "Babar and Celeste," and began to read to them of a delightful world of gentle good manners, where elephants and people find happiness together, they became loyal listeners and then, avid readers. When they entered kindergarten, Mrs. Segal picked up where Mrs. Simmons left off, and read "Where the Wild Things Are" and "Charlotte's Web." I wonder if either of these dedicated storytellers knows of the profound effect they have had on the children of our town.

The Storysmith

* * * * * * * * *

"Irene is a natural!" Miranda told Joseph. "She's learned our routine in no time at all."

Miranda divided Ruthie's responsibilities among the four of them—Irene, Danny, Melanie and herself. By the time the next Sunday evening rolled around, they were a team; and with Joseph as host and cashier, Miranda was reasonably sure that the evening would go smoothly.

After the dishes were cleared and coffee poured, Miranda stepped up to the microphone.

"Ladies and gentlemen, it is my pleasure to introduce our second finalist, Emma Siegal. Some of you may remember Mrs. Siegal from her days as a kindergarten teacher at Dos Hermanas Elementary School. She's been retired for a while now, but has kept active with our local theater group. Let's give her a warm welcome."

They applauded as a tiny old woman with short gray hair made her way toward the fireplace. Although she moved slowly, her back was very straight. She held her head high and smiled. She wore a plain light blue blouse with a navy skirt, stockings and shoes. A cameo brooch was fastened at her throat and small gold earrings completed her outfit.

As she came up to the storyteller's stool, it became obvious that she would need help to get up on it. She turned toward the audience and looked out at them. Her bright blue eyes searched from table to table until she spotted the face she was looking for.

"Matthew Sanders, you were the biggest and strongest boy in your class. Will you help me up?"

A tall husky young man in his mid thirties stood and answered,

"Yes Ma'am, Mrs. Siegal. It's my pleasure, Ma'am."

He came forward and gently lifted her onto the stool. The crowd rewarded him with a small burst of laughter and applause. Matthew took a bow with one hand across his waist in front and the other in back, just the way he had been taught in Mrs. Siegal's kindergarten class.

"I'll lift you down when you are ready, Ma'am," he said and returned to his seat.

"Thank you, Matthew," she replied gravely.

After settling herself comfortably on the stool and adjusting the microphone, Emma looked up and surveyed her audience.

"Matthew isn't the only one I recognize this evening," she commented, dryly.

Everyone laughed. She had taught many of the old-timers in town when they were five, but had not been shy about admonishing them when they misbehaved in public, even when they were teens, college aged, and older.

"Tonight, I'm going to tell you a love story," she began, "and if you think you recognize any of the characters, let me assure you, they are purely fictional and a product of too much time on my hands and an active imagination.

"In the great metropolis of Los Angeles, there dwelt a charming lady named Sarah Friedman. Sarah was a widow. Her beloved husband, Samuel, had gone to his heavenly reward three years ago. After a suitable mourning period, Sarah had made a comfortable life for herself visiting her four children and six grandchildren, volunteering at the local hospital and reading racy historical novels.

"She had recently celebrated her seventy fifth birthday. As a birthday gift, her four grown children had chipped in and presented her with a one-week cruise to Cabo San Lucas. It left from Los Angeles, so she wouldn't need to fly, which she had never done and had not the slightest desire to start now.

"'Thank you, kindly!' Sarah responded to their generous gift, 'but vat should an old lady like me do on a cruise?'

"'Go, Mom, you'll have a nice time,' they insisted. 'You can go for walks and play cards, and be waited on hand and foot. You can go shopping in Mexico. You'll love it!'

"Sarah breathed a deep sign of resignation. 'Well, all right then, I'll go if it makes you happy, but I still don't know vat I could possibly do on a boat all by myself...Well, maybe I'll have a good rest and read a few romance novels.'

"So she packed her bags, got her hair freshly waved and a manicure. Her children took her to San Pedro, where the cruise ships docked, and saw to it that she was safely ensconced in her closet-sized cabin aboard 'The Viking Serenade.'

"'Some stupid name for a boat,' she grumbled. 'Who ever heard of a Viking serenading, anyvay? If vun of those barbarians stood outside my vindow bellowing some Svedish love song, you can believe me, he'd get a pot of hot water on his head soon enough!'

"She sat down on the narrow bed and removed her shoes. She put on socks and 'Reeboks' and went out to explore the ship. When 'first call to dinner' was announced, she found the main dining room and was shown to her table. As she sat down, she noticed a folded card identifying this table as #18.

"At that moment, as if preordained, a slight, bookish-looking man approached Sarah and asked, 'Excuse me, Missus, is this table eighteen?'

'Yes, it certainly is,' replied Sarah.

'Oh, then this is my table, too. May I join you?'

"'Please do,' replied Sarah, 'My name is Sarah Friedman and I live in Los Angeles.'

"'Pleased to meet you, Mrs. Friedman. My name is Fred Schwartz and I'm from Chicago...In the poultry business.'

"'Pleased to make your acqvuaintance, Mr. Schvartz,' said Sarah.

"'Oh, please call me "Fred"'" he replied. 'A cruise is no place to be formal. We have only one week to get acquainted.'

"Sarah looked at Fred and smiled. She was pleased with what she saw.

"'Vhat a nice face,' she thought. 'Such an intelligent look about him…and such a sveet smile.'

"As Fred gazed at Sarah, he felt a warmth radiating from a spot in his chest straight out to his fingers and toes.

"'My God, what's happening to me?' he thought, 'Am I a teen ager that I should feel like this all of a sudden?'

"Sarah and Fred chatted cheerfully all through dinner. They talked about their lives in Los Angeles and Chicago. Later, they danced in the main ballroom until the bandleader turned on the muzak. It seemed the most natural thing in the world when Fred walked Sarah to her cabin and kissed her cheek, as if they were already old friends.

"From then on, Sarah and Fred were inseparable. Day and night, they were together. They ate and talked, danced and talked, shopped and talked, went sightseeing and talked, but most of all, they talked. They talked about everything, anything and nothing.

"'Oh dear, if my children should see me now,' thought Sarah, as she woke up one morning in Fred's arms, 'What would they think of their foolish old mother?' she clucked softly to herself."

"Then she smiled, turned over and closed her eyes for 'just fifty vinks more.'

"Too soon, the cruise ended. As they prepared to disembark in Los Angeles, Sarah and Fred exchanged addresses and spoke of getting together for another cruise. It was time to get back to reality. Sarah lived in Los Angeles and Fred lived in Chicago, 'and that vas that!'

"A few weeks later, Sarah went to the drugstore to pick up the snapshots she had taken aboard 'The Viking

Serenade.' As she gazed at each photo, she and Fred having a wonderful time together, she felt a sudden pang of loneliness. She sighed deeply.

"'I didn't think I vould miss him so soon. It's only been a couple of veeks…Maybe,' she thought, 'Maybe I'll give him a call, just to say "Hello."'

"She went to look for the slip of paper on which Fred had written his address and phone number, but it was nowhere to be found. Finally, she shook her head and sighed, 'I can't believe I could be so careless! I can't remember vere I could have put it. Oh, vell, never mind. He told me he vorks for the Apex Poultry Company in Chicago. So I'll get the number from "Information."'

"Sarah dialed Chicago Information and, sure enough, The Apex Poultry Company was listed. She wrote the number neatly in her little red address book. Then, she picked up the receiver once more and dialed the number.

"'Di, diddle dee diddle dum dum dee' she sang to herself as she waited for someone to answer. The operator greeted her politely:

"'Apex Poultry Company, Good Afternoon. How may I direct your call?'

"'Yes, dear, this is Sarah Friedman. I'm calling long distance from Los Angeles. May I speak with Mr. Fred Schwartz, please?'

"There was a short pause and then the pleasant voice of the receptionist informed her, 'I'm sorry Ma'am, but I do not find anyone by that name listed.'

"'Are you sure, dear?' asked Sarah. 'He's such a nice man. He told me that he works at your company. I'm sure he vouldn't say it if it vasn't so.'

Miranda's Muse

"'Well, it is possible that Mr. Schwartz works for one of our other divisions. Can you hold on, Mrs. Friedman while I check the company roster?'

"Yes, dear, I vill and thank you for your trouble.'

"The operator pressed her 'hold' button and a cheerful tune played to ease Sarah's wait. Sarah began to hum along with the music and idled away the few minutes it took for the operator to come back on the line.

"'Mrs. Friedman, I found a Mr. Fred Schwartz in our specialty poultry division.'

"'Oh, he's a specialist? I didn't know. Could you connect me, dear?'

"'I'm afraid everyone has left for the weekend, Mrs. Friedman.'

"'Oh, yes, that's right. Chicago is two hours ahead of Los Angeles. Could you give me his home phone number, please? I lost the piece of paper I wrote it down on.'

"'I'm sorry, Ma'am, but it's against company policy to give out our employees' telephone numbers.'

"'Well, can I leave a message for him?' asked Sarah.

"'Yes, Ma'am, if you'll give me your phone number, I'll see that Mr. Schwartz gets it when he comes to work on Monday morning.'

"Sarah left her number with the Apex Poultry Company operator, and replaced the receiver in its cradle.

'I can hardly vait to talk to him,' she thought to herself. 'Who vould've thought that an old woman of seventy-five and a man of seventy two could fall in love? …at least, I think Fred loves me. He told me so at least five times on our cruise.'

"Sarah tried to keep herself busy over the weekend, so she wouldn't dwell on Fred's phone call. Monday dawned bright and sunny and Sarah awoke to the thought that today Fred would call. She got up, did her morning stretches and then busied herself dusting and setting her house to rights.

"By noon, Fred had not yet called, so Sarah decided to bake some cookies so she'd have some on hand when her grandchildren came to see her. She baked three different kinds…chocolate chip, oatmeal raisin and lemon bars, but still Fred did not call.

"'Maybe, he couldn't call from vork,' she told herself, 'so, he'll call later, maybe five o'clock Los Angeles time; that vould be seven in Chicago.'

"But when her clock chimed seven o'clock, time for 'Jeopardy,' her favorite TV show, Sarah knew that Fred would not call tonight.

"'Maybe he's sick, God forbid, and didn't get my message.'

"Sarah tried not to make too much of it, but she couldn't help feeling disappointed.

"'Look at you,' she said to her reflection in the mirror, 'Carrying on like a sixteen year old because your boyfriend didn't call! You should know better.'

"By Tuesday afternoon, Sarah began to fret.

"'Maybe it was only a shipboard romance, after all. But to me, it was a miracle. I never expected to love another man after my Sam died.'

"By Thursday morning, Sarah was calling herself a fool for believing that love could come to two people in their seventies.

"'So maybe it's because Fred is younger than me. Maybe he doesn't vant to take a chance with a woman three years older.'

"But somehow, Sarah knew in her heart that this wasn't true. They had found such joy with each other. Surely, a man like Fred couldn't fake that. Sarah was old enough and wise enough to know if someone was sincere or not.

"'Well, tomorrow is Valentine's Day. I bet he was vaiting until then. That would be just like Fred, to be so sentimental. Okay, if I don't get a card or a call by tomorrow, I'll call Apex Poultry again.' She resolved not to think about it any more tonight.

"February fourteenth turned out to be a gray and cloudy day. Rain seemed imminent, but Los Angeles is like that; it could look like rain for weeks on end and never drop so much as one little raindrop. Sarah rose and dressed herself in a new dusty rose outfit she had bought at 'Ross Dress for Less.' After she had put on a little soft pink lipstick and her pearl earrings, she checked her appearance in the mirror.

"'So, not too shabby for an old lady,' she decided.

"Sarah went into the kitchen to start breakfast. After popping a bagel into the toaster and plugging in her coffee pot, she set a place at the table. She put a place mat down where she could see out of the window as she ate. She set out a jar of guava jelly and a tub of cream cheese. As she folded a napkin and placed it by her plate, she remembered how her mother had always been amused when young Sarah would set a place for herself, even if no one else were going to be home. Setting a place for one seemed very strange to some folks, Sarah reflected, but she had always felt that it was important to do this for herself. It was a question of self-respect.

"Just then the doorbell rang. Sarah went to open the door. A deliveryman stood in her doorway, carrying a large pink Azalea plant.

"'Oh, my, how beautiful!' she exclaimed and showed the boy where to set it down. After signing his book and tipping him a dollar, she closed the door behind him and went to admire the plant once more.

"'See, you foolish old lady,' she scolded herself, 'You didn't need to vorry like that, as if Fred would forget you!'

"Sarah sat down on the sofa and reached for the card which came with Fred's gift. When she opened it, she saw that it wasn't just a florist's gift card, but a letter that had been sent to accompany the azalea.

"'Dear Sarah,' the letter began, 'I know you won't mind my calling you by your first name. You see, I feel as if I already know you. My father, Fred Schwartz returned from his cruise to Mexico bubbling over with happiness. He told us he'd met a wonderful and beautiful woman and that he'd fallen head over heels in love with her. As you can imagine, my sister and I were very surprised. Dad had grieved so deeply for our mother that we were afraid that he would never recover from her death.

"'We want you to know how happy we are that our father met and fell in love with you. That week that you and Dad spent together aboard "The Viking Serenade" was the happiest week of his life since our mother died. He was planning to send you these flowers on Valentine's Day along with a proposal of marriage.'

"Sarah put down the letter for a moment and gazed at the beautiful flowers,

"'I knew it! He loves me, too…Marriage…Oh, my! I never thought…"

"Then she picked up the letter and read further:

"'Instead, I am sending them. Sadly, my father will not be able to live out his dream of spending the rest of his life with you. He went to bed at ten o'clock on the tenth of February, happily making plans for bringing you to Chicago to meet his grandchildren and us. When he did not answer my early morning phone call, I went to check on him. I let myself into his apartment and found him still in bed. He looked relaxed and rosy, a smile on his lips. Only he was not asleep. He was gone. He must have died only a short while before I got there, the doctor said, from a massive stroke. We thank God he did not suffer.'

"'Although we will miss him greatly, we are grateful that his last days on earth were so wonderful. Thank you, Sarah, for making our father so happy.'

"The letter was signed, 'With love, Sylvia and Lorraine, daughters of Fred Schwartz.'

"As Sarah finished reading the letter, tears welled up and spilled over. She sat quietly weeping until she had to go for a clean hanky to wipe her eyes and blow her nose. She brought a glass of water back to the sofa with her and sipped it until she was calm. Then she poured the remainder into the Azalea plant and leaned back against the sofa cushions. When she closed her eyes, she could visualize Fred and herself together on shipboard, smiling, dancing and having a great time. After a while, Sarah fell asleep.

"She didn't know exactly how long she had slept, but when she awoke, she saw the beautiful pink Azalea on the coffee table and smiled sadly.

"'Well, I suppose the Almighty had other plans. So, nu!' she said, looking to heaven, 'Vat vould've it hurt to let him live a few days longer? Never mind; sometimes, talking to You is like talking to myself!'

Arlene Spector

"' So! Anyway, I vouldn't have missed knowing Fred for anything,' she told herself. 'It's not every day that a woman my age receives such an honor…a shipboard romance and a proposal of marriage, too! I guess I'll have to be satisfied with that.'

"She took the Azalea to the kitchen sink and gave it some more water. Then she placed it on the kitchen table, where she could look at it while she ate. She spread cream cheese on her bagel, and then spread her favorite guava jelly on extra thick.

"'That's life, Sarah, you old fool,' she chided herself. 'Just ven things go right, you can expect the unexpected. Hmph!'

"Sarah sat idly over the remains of her breakfast and gazed out of the window. She noticed that the Indian Hawthorne bushes were already blooming and the camellias were just beginning to fade. There were oranges on the tree, but they weren't quite orange enough to be sweet.

"'I guess spring showed up here in Los Angeles ven I vasn't paying attention,' she mused…So, maybe…maybe I should go on another cruise…'"

* * * * * * * * *

Emma paused and smiled at her audience.

"And that, my dears, is the end of my story, although it may be the beginning of another for Sarah."

There were smiles on many faces, but a few people wiped tears from their eyes before they applauded.

"Now, Matthew, if you don't mind…"

The big man made his way toward the tiny woman, lifted her down and set Emma on her feet. As she received the applause of her listeners, Emma made a little curtsy and went to rejoin her table. Matthew did likewise.

Miranda came forward and stood by the microphone.

"Thank you, Emma. That was a lovely story."

CHAPTER SEVEN

"It is important to remember the spiritual context of a meal;" said Rabbi Kamrass, in his Talmudic commentary on Deuteronomy 8: 10. "In Judaism, the table is an altar and the food is an indication of God's blessing."

When Miranda prepared food, she would bow her head and meditate for a few moments, in respect for the divine gift of the ingredients before her. When she was asked what was the secret of her excellent cuisine, she replied:

"Never do anything to mask the true nature of the food you prepare. Choose only the finest and freshest fruits and vegetables, and treat them gently and reverently, as though the meal you prepare is for The Goddess Herself. Anything less is blasphemy."

The Storysmith

* * * * * * * * *

On Tuesday morning, Danny and Miranda arrived at the cafe together. They parked in their usual places and met at the back door of the cafe just as Miranda was turning the key in the lock.

"G'morning, Miranda!" Danny's voice was cheerful even this early in the morning, Miranda noticed. She nodded her response, and swung the door open. Some people were clearly morning people, she reflected, while others needed that first cup of coffee to be truly awake. They marched silently into the kitchen and hung their sweaters on the hooks behind the door. Miranda poured herself a cup of coffee from the big urn and took a sip. Then she poured Danny a cup. Finally, she was ready to begin the workday.

"Good morning, Danny. How was your weekend?" she asked courteously, hoping that he would not go into excruciating detail, at least until she had finished that first cup of coffee.

However, he seemed to sense her mood and replied briefly, "It was okay, I guess. How was yours?"

"Fine," she replied, and began to fill the big electric kettle. Danny nodded and went to start the gas griddle.

As Miranda and Danny worked silently, she noticed how comfortable it felt to work in tandem this way. He knew the cafe's routine well and he worked quickly and efficiently, somehow knowing exactly where Miranda was and where she would move next. He accommodated to her work style so easily, she wasn't sure that he was even aware of it. They never bumped into each other or needed the same utensil at the same time. It made work a pleasure.

As Miranda mused on this phenomenon, she realized that the joy she felt in working this way was the same feeling she had when she and Joseph danced together. They had been dancing partners for almost forty years and each knew the other's style, movements and preferences instinctively. Sometimes when the band was playing "golden oldies," Miranda would ask Joseph to allow her to call the steps for a while. He would oblige her easily as she whispered "French dip," for once referring not to the popular sandwich, but to a dramatic dance step from their youth. Occasionally, she would tell Joseph, "I'm tired of dancing backwards," and he would good naturally relinquish the lead while maintaining classic dance position.

Of course, Danny's role was to follow her lead at work and accommodate to her movements. In this way, Miranda decided, it was really more like ballet, with the male partner standing by to lift, twirl, or otherwise support the dancing of the prima ballerina. She was amused by her own conceit, and started humming the Swan Queen's theme from "Swan Lake."

Danny smiled when he heard Miranda humming to herself. It was great working with someone as cheerful and competent as Miranda, he thought. He opened the refrigerator door and took out eggs and placed them at the ready for the first order of bacon and eggs. Somehow, the most mundane work became fun when things hummed along this smoothly, "No pun intended," he said to himself, and grinned.

Just then, the bell connected to the front door rang. Miranda went to greet her first customer of the day.

As she pushed through the swinging door, Miranda saw two women sitting at a table near the window. They were studying their menus as Miranda walked up to their table.

"Good morning, Ladies. What can I get for you?" she asked.

When they put their menus down, the older of the two smiled at Miranda and greeted her.

"How nice to see you, Miranda. It must be ages since we last met." she said, and Miranda recognized her old friend, Jean McCullough.

"Jean, my goodness, you look terrific! ...And who is this young lady? Don't tell me it's your daughter. The last time I remember seeing her she was a tiny wisp of a thing. Surely it can't have been that long!"

"Yes, indeed," replied Jean. "Miranda, I'd like to present my daughter, Tanya. Tanya, this is Miranda, owner and manager of Miranda's Cafe and a very good friend of mine."

Tanya was a very unusual looking young woman. Miranda thought she must be around twenty-one or two. She was Eurasian, the product of her Asian mother and a father from a Scotch-Irish family. There was a strange look about her, sort of exotic, in Miranda's judgment. Her hair, which she wore pulled back in a ponytail, was a Titian red. Her eyes were an unearthly sea green. Her complexion was pale and of a most unusual shade…a mixture of tan and pale ochre, with a sprinkling of freckles across the bridge of her nose. There was a discordant quality about the young woman. She didn't seem comfortable in the bright and cheerful atmosphere of the cafe. She was restless and tapped nervously on the tabletop with her long fingernails. Miranda took their order and went back into the kitchen to prepare their hot cakes and sausages.

"Danny, why don't you pour coffee for our guests? I'll bring their hot cakes as soon as they're ready."

He filled a carafe with coffee from the urn, took a cream pitcher from the refrigerator and went into the dining room. Miranda could hear his pleasant young voice bantering with Jean and Tanya as he poured coffee.

As she worked, Miranda thought back to the first time she met Jean. It was at a women's conference at the college. There were numerous seminars for the participants to choose from, and Miranda selected one entitled "Know Thyself." She had found this title amusing, wondering if it was about Shakespeare's famous speech by Polonius in

"Hamlet," or perhaps a treatise on biblical autoeroticism. She gave herself a mental slap on the wrist for her bad pun.

The class began with everyone choosing a partner and interviewing her. In turn, they switched roles and the interviewee became the interviewer. When they were through, they were to introduce their partners to the class. Somehow, Miranda and Jean had ended up as partners, and they went off together to find a peaceful spot on campus where they could conduct their interviews.

Miranda wondered whether she'd be able to elicit much from Jean. Jean seemed shy to Miranda, or at least very reserved. When Jean introduced herself, Miranda was startled and burst out, "Jean McCullough? Somehow you just don't look like my picture of a Scotswoman," and she chuckled.

Jean smiled and answered: "I hope you're not disappointed. Who did you expect?"

"I guess I was picturing a tall, angular person with red hair and strong features, wearing good tweeds and sensible oxfords."

Jean certainly didn't fit that description. She was small, Asian, and fashionably dressed in beautifully tailored slacks, a silk shirt and checked blazer.

"Well, so much for preconceived notions!" and the two women laughed merrily.

"I'm fascinated. How did you get to be who you are?" asked Miranda.

Jean told her that she'd been born to a Japanese family who had immigrated to California when they were young, become citizens, and raised a family here. Jean got her degree in psychology. She met and married an American of

Scotch-Irish background and later gave birth to Tanya, her only child.

That explained her name, but at first Jean didn't seem inclined to say much more. Instead she started asking Miranda about her own background. She was a good listener and skillful in asking thought provoking questions to keep Miranda on track.

Miranda told all about her family and what it was like growing up in New York City. Jean was particularly interested in the story of how Miranda's mother had single-handedly arranged for almost one hundred Jewish refugees from Nazi Germany to find sanctuary in the United States.

"How did that effect you, Miranda?" asked Jean. Miranda thought about it for a minute or two before answering.

"It's a strange thing, but I just accepted the situation as normal. It never occurred to me that other families did not usually have cots set up in their living rooms for refugees to sleep on until someone like my mother found them jobs, places to live and occasionally, spouses."

"I have a theory," Miranda continued. "I think children will accept whatever circumstances they find themselves in as a given, because they have never known anything else."

Jean thought that was an interesting idea. "It certainly holds true for me," she responded.

"In what way?" asked Miranda.

Jean looked hesitant about saying more, so Miranda asked boldly, "Jean, how old are you?"

Jean looked surprised, so Miranda quickly proffered her own age to take the onus off the question. As it turned out, Jean was only a few years older than Miranda.

"You are probably the right age to have been part of the relocation of Japanese-Americans to internment camps during World War II."

Jean's face tightened and she answered softly, "Yes, I was."

She seemed to want to drop the subject right there, but Miranda could no longer retreat.

"I'd consider it an honor to hear about your life then. It was a shameful thing for America, and I cannot imagine how you coped with it."

Jean was still for what seemed a long time to Miranda. Her normally smooth, composed features were working as she thought back to Manzanar, the infamous California detention camp.

Finally, Jean spoke.

"You know, Miranda, I've never spoken of that time to anyone, not even my husband."

"You don't have to, Jean, if you'd rather not."

"No, I think it's time that I did, and you seem to be the right person to tell."

And so, Jean McCullough, the daughter of immigrant Japanese produce farmers from Fresno began to tell her story to Miranda, the daughter of German-Jewish refugees from the holocaust. Miranda was spellbound as she listened to Jean's quiet, unembellished story.

"My father came to the United States by himself in 1924. He had signed up to work as stoop labor in the farmlands of the central valley of California. It was back breaking hard work, but he didn't complain. Instead, he saved every penny he earned so that he could send for my mother, a young woman who had been chosen by his parents to be his wife. He had met her only once or twice before he left Japan, but he was confident that they could make their way in this new country together. They were married the day she stepped off the boat in San Francisco.

"By this time, he had saved just enough money to purchase a small patch of land near Fresno. So, they began their life together in the tiny shack he had been able to build with his own two hands. They worked hard together, planting and tending their vegetable fields and they were able to reap a bumper crop, which they sold to restaurants in San Francisco's China Town. It was not too long after that, that my parents started a family. I, and my six brothers and sisters came along within a year or two of each other. Everything seemed to be going well for our family until December 7, 1941. Not long after that, we suddenly found ourselves looked upon as 'enemy aliens.' even though my parents had by this time become American citizens. It had been one of the proudest days of their lives, and now, the nation they loved betrayed them.

"To make a long and ugly story short, we were forced to sell our farm for almost nothing, and we were rounded up like cattle and sent to an internment camp—we thought of it as a concentration camp. No, we were not tortured, unless forcing the nine of us to live in two tiny rooms in a converted chicken coop qualifies as torture. We girls slept in one room with our mother, while my father and brothers shared the other room."

As the facts came out, one by one, Miranda could feel her throat tightening and tears welling beneath her eyelids.

"Were your parents bitter?" Miranda asked.

"N-no," Jean started to reply. Then she changed her mind.

"Yes, they were very bitter; my father more than my mother. I think it broke his heart. He had been such a patriot. He loved this country with a passion stronger than anything else I can think of, and it let him down in the worst possible way."

"How did you and your brothers and sisters deal with it?" asked Miranda.

Jean took a big breath and let it out slowly.

"We learned to hate being of Japanese ancestry. All seven of us married Anglos, as though that would make us more American. It took years of therapy to get over that. Some of my siblings were not so lucky. They still suffer the effects."

"Did the twenty-thousand dollar reparations money from the government help at all?" asked Miranda.

"In a way," replied Jean. "It wasn't so much the money itself, as it was the apology that helped. But even that couldn't heal our invisible wounds."

Jean fell silent. Her eyes filled with tears and she let them run unheeded down her cheeks. Miranda, too, wept and she took Jean's hand in her own. Jean nodded and returned the loving squeeze. At that moment, the Nisei woman and the Jewish woman had come closer to one another than either of them could ever have predicted.

* * * * * * * * *

The hot cakes and sausages were ready. Miranda pushed through the swinging doors backward with a plate in each hand. She set them down in front of Jean and Tanya, and turned to go back to the kitchen.

Miranda's Muse

"Miranda, couldn't you sit down and have a cup of coffee with us? There's something I'd like to ask you."

"Sure, but let me tell Danny, so he can wait on patrons. I don't have long, as you can guess. I expect my breakfast regulars any time now."

When Miranda returned to Jean's table, she had brought her coffee mug with her.

"You said there was something you wanted to talk about?"

"Yes, it concerns Tanya. I brought her to meet you for a special reason. She received her degree last June in Journalism, and she just landed her first job."

"Congratulations, Tanya, I wish you the best of luck."

"Thanks," murmured Tanya, the first word she'd spoken since coming in.

"Why don't you take over from here, Tanya, and tell Miranda what you have in mind," her mother prompted.

Tanya breathed a large sigh.

"Okay. I'm going to be working for a Fort Bragg paper. It's called 'The Braggart.' My mother thinks it'll be a good idea to write a story about your short story contest."

"And what do you think, Tanya?" asked Miranda.

"I guess it is. I mean we don't exactly have a lot of juicy gossip going around, do we? And it sure beats stories like, 'Mrs. Mary Brown' entertains the church ladies for tea at her lovely home in Dos Hermanas.'"

Miranda laughed, "You're right, Tanya, we don't have many scandals her in Dos Hermanas. I guess that's why I make up stories and tell them here at the cafe. I can create wild and improbable situations; people enjoy them and no harm to anyone. We all know it's fiction. In any case, you're welcome to attend the rest of the contest presentations, and if you'd like to read the two you've missed, that can be arranged."

"Thank you so much, Miranda. See, Tanya, I told you she'd agree," said Jean.

"Sure," said Miranda, "And dinner on the house is included. Of course, you won't be able to vote for the winner, since you didn't hear all the stories."

"Okay," said Tanya, and finished the last of her hot cakes.

Just then, the doorbell tinkled again. Miranda looked up and waved a greeting to two of her breakfast regulars.

"Duty calls," she remarked cheerfully.

Jean rose from her chair and the two women hugged each other.

"I do appreciate your generosity, Miranda," said Jean softly, "Tanya hasn't had an easy time of it."

Miranda nodded, "I hope you and I can get together again soon, Jean."

"Me, too," replied Jean. "There's lots to talk about."

As Miranda returned to the kitchen, she noticed that Danny had already poured coffee and was just taking down the breakfast order for Mr. and Mrs. O'Brien, an elderly couple who had been coming in for breakfast two or three days a week for the past twenty years. She smiled and waved at them on her way past.

As she came through the swinging doors, she let out a large sigh and shook her head from side to side.

"That child makes me nervous," she thought to herself, "and I don't know why."

That evening, after checking that all the doors were securely locked, Miranda started out on the familiar road home. Her notebook lay beside her on the passenger seat as usual, the ballpoint pen clipped to its cover. But tonight Miranda couldn't summon up the energy to analyze the day's work and make notes to herself as to what she needed to do tomorrow. She couldn't remember feeling so bone weary since the children had grown up and begun lives of their own.

"I guess this is what growing old is all about," she thought. "I don't snap back as quickly as I did when I was younger...I seemed to have an inexhaustible supply of energy then."

She dwelled on this thought briefly. By then, she had reached a place along the road that afforded a magnificent view of the tree covered rolling hills which lay between Dos Hermanas and the ocean. On a whim, Miranda pulled the little truck over to the right and parked. She climbed out of the cab and walked toward the outer edge of the shoulder, where it touched a wooded area with a beautiful copse of evergreens and oak trees. As she did, the moon came out from partial concealment behind a cloud, and shone brightly on the scene below and beyond.

It was absolutely still; not a whisper of a breeze touched the leaves and needles of the trees. Miranda realized that she was holding her breath so as not to disturb the serenity of this moment. She took a breath and allowed the scent of pine with a trace of kelp from the sea to enter her lungs. She held it in until she could hold it no longer, and then slowly she exhaled and felt herself relax.

At that moment, Miranda became aware that she was not alone. She could sense the presence of someone or something observing her from her right side. It felt like a slight warm tingling on her right arm and her cheek. Slowly, she turned to face whatever it was. At first, she could only make out the dark shadows of the trees. Then, from the edge of the forest, something moved slowly into Miranda's field of vision. She froze motionless where she was and waited.

The full moon moved out from the edge of a cloud formation and lit the clearing as brightly as daylight. There, sitting erect, with both pointed ears on alert, was a canine. At first, Miranda thought it was a German shepherd, but as the creature raised its head, Miranda could see clear golden eyes in a stern gray and buff face with black markings and an overlay of white around the muzzle.

"It's a wolf," she realized.

There were not many wolves left in this area, but Miranda had heard of occasional sightings, especially near the mountains.

Miranda sensed that the wolf was not out to harm her, so she waited quietly for the wolf to make her first move. They gazed at each other, the woman and the wolf. Neither of them seemed the least bit nervous or fearful. Miranda broke the silence.

"Good evening, Comrade Wolf," she said, in a quiet conversational tone, "I see you have come to take in the beauty of the night, even as I have. You are welcome."

The wolf cocked her head to one side and allowed her mouth to relax and her wet pink tongue to slip easily out over her lower teeth. She seemed to be smiling. Miranda smiled back and licked her lips and the wolf seemed to relax even more. She rose and stretched her body, planting her hind legs out behind her and elongating her spine toward her shoulders. She yawned and began to approach Miranda. Miranda stood very still and waited.

Finally, the wolf was standing beside her, with her alert, intelligent face tilted up to look into Miranda's eyes. Miranda could see now that this was indeed an old she wolf. The white frosting on her muzzle was clearly the "graying" of her thick coat.

"Well," said Miranda, "here we are, you and I, Sister Wolf, two old ladies looking at the moon. Perhaps you've been thinking of times gone by, just as I have. The wolf moved her tail slowly as if in agreement. Then, she turned to face the hills and valleys and sat down at Miranda's feet. Together they gazed out on the peaceful moonlit hills and let the comfort of a kindred spirit enhance their pleasure in the scene. At that moment, the old she wolf raised her muzzle high and howled a long, plaintive cry. She repeated this several times with minor variations in tone. Then she paused and looked at Miranda expectantly. Miranda looked deeply into the beautiful golden eyes and then, she too, tilted her head back and howled at the moon. The she wolf picked up the cue and together, the old woman and the old wolf sang their primeval hymn to the moon.

Finally, when the moon had again hidden behind a cloud, Miranda turned to her lupine companion, but the wolf had already slipped into the woods.

"Thank you, Sister Wolf, thank you," she called softly.

A little later, after Miranda had turned into her driveway and switched off the motor, she sat for a moment thinking of what had happened.

"You're a crazy old woman, Miranda!" she told herself, "who howls at the moon with the wolves...truly a 'lunatic'. I think you'd better keep this to yourself, you nut!"

She nodded her head and then burst into laughter,

"No problem," she said aloud. "Who would believe it, anyway?"

CHAPTER EIGHT

Once upon a time, in the city of Prague, the chief Rabbi of the old synagogue feared the rising tide of virulent anti-Semitism among the local gentiles. So, the story goes, he modeled a figure resembling a large and powerful man. Then he prayed night and day, with all the power that was in him, that God would breathe the breath of life into "The Golem," as the figure was called. His wish was granted and the Golem was hidden in the cellars of the old synagogue, until a mob of hooligans threatened to burn down the synagogue as well as the frightened people who had sought refuge within the sacred walls.

The Golem was brought out of the cellars and, because he was a Golem, not a human being, he could not be killed. Instead he went out against the mob and did terrible damage among them, thereby saving the old synagogue and all those who had sought refuge there. It is said that the Golem still sleeps deep within the cellars of the old Synagogue, in case he may be needed again.

The Storysmith

*   *   *   *   *   *   *   *   *

Miranda surveyed the scene in the dining room. The diners were talking and laughing among themselves. The weather had turned nippy this evening and people had bundled up a bit more than usual. The bright colors of their sweaters added to the cheerful ambiance.

Arlene Spector

Miranda spotted Tanya McCullough sitting at one of the back tables. In contrast to the brightly colored clothing of the others, Tanya was dressed all in black and wore no make up; her hair was pulled back severely and twisted into a tight bun on the back of her head. She stuck out like a crow in a flock of parrots, thought Miranda.

Tanya sat silently watching the goings on, and occasionally checking her watch. She looked bored and sat tapping restlessly on the table.

"It's amazing how different a child can be from her mother," thought Miranda. "It's not surprising that Tanya hasn't had an easy time of it."

Miranda remembered one of Momma's favorite expressions: "The way you look is the way you will be received."

The picture of herself that Tanya presented was not one that would elicit a positive response; of that Miranda was certain.

When the hubbub had subsided somewhat, Miranda began the evening's festivities.

"Ladies and gentlemen, welcome to our third story contest presentation. Tonight, we are privileged to hear a story by Luisa Marino, our third finalist. Let's welcome Luisa."

The audience applauded enthusiastically as Luisa made her way to the microphone. She was well known to most of the locals as an RN at Dos Hermanas Hospital, where she presided over the newborn nursery. She had personally welcomed many of Dos Hermanas' children into the world.

This evening, she had traded her nurse's uniform for a long sleeved dress with a cheerful print of small rose-colored flowers on a navy blue background. A lovely antique lace collar adorned the high neck of her dress, and Luisa wore her grandmother's small drop pearl earrings "for luck," she told her husband, Ernie.

Luisa was a small, slender woman with dark hair and olive skin reminiscent of her Neapolitan forbears. Her large very dark eyes and straight bold eyebrows reminded Miranda of a Byzantine Madonna she once saw at a San Francisco art museum.

Luisa settled herself comfortably on the storyteller's stool by the fireplace and adjusted the microphone. When she was ready, she folded her hands in her lap, and looked around the room from table to table, acknowledging with her gaze the familiar faces of friends, neighbors and former patients. She smiled and wished them all.

"Good evening."

They murmured their greetings in return and waited expectantly for Luisa to begin her story.

"I am about to tell you a story about two dear friends of ours from the past. It is a strange tale in that they never actually met, nor did they ever have so much as a phone conversation. Had my husband and I not been the connecting link between them, what happened later would never have come to pass.

"I call my story 'The Engineer and the Witch,' because that's exactly who they were. I shall call the engineer 'Dwight Singer' and the witch 'Margo Aguilar.' I have used fictitious names with good reason, as you will see when you know all the facts.

"Now, as you can probably guess, engineers and witches are very different from one another. An engineer is a person who believes that most problems can be solved through a careful application of logic. Whatever happens can be explained by a rational analysis of the facts; and the science of mathematics provides the most trustworthy tools for the job. Dwight was fond of saying: 'If I can't see it, touch it, taste it, smell it or hear it, and if I can't measure it or prove it by scientific means, it's hogwash.'

"Margo, on the other hand, knew for certain that the world we perceive with our five senses is only a small part of creation. Spirits, ghosts, poltergeists, gremlins and other supernatural beings were an everyday part of her life, whereas Dwight placed these so-called 'psychic phenomena' in the province of fools and children. A witch was an imaginary creature who rode a broomstick on Halloween and not to be taken any more seriously than that.

"Now I wouldn't want you to get the impression that Dwight was all work and no play. On the contrary, we found him to be a pleasant companion, well read and able to hold his own in social settings. We often invited him over for potluck after he and Ernie, my husband, were through with work for the day. He seemed to enjoy my plain home cooking and used to tease me by asking where he could find a woman just like me to marry. That's the kind of compliment you get after you're safely married to someone else!

"Once, Dwight decided to reciprocate for the many dinners he'd enjoyed at our house. He would cook Mother's Day dinner for me. Since his place was too cramped for company, he asked to do it at our home and to invite another friend along. Of course, we agreed. Dwight further stipulated that I was not to lift a finger to help. He would do the marketing, cook the dinner, set the table and clean up afterwards. How could I refuse?

"On Mother's Day, Dwight showed up at three o'clock in the afternoon. He carried in two large grocery bags overflowing with good things. He set them down in the kitchen and tried to shoo me out of there. After some fast-talking on my part, however, I was able to persuade him to allow me to watch.

"Ernie had often remarked that Dwight had such 'good hands' in the laboratory. This was my chance to see for myself what he meant. Dwight selected several perfect tomatoes, green peppers, large sweet onions, eggplants and zucchini. Then he took a sharp knife and prepared them to be stuffed. I have never seen anyone so deft with a kitchen knife. He moved with surgical precision! Then he prepared the stuffing of chopped lamb and rice, browned together and seasoned with garlic and other spices. He stuffed each of the vegetables and then fitted their tops back on so perfectly, I couldn't have told that they were ever cut.

"Dwight placed the stuffed vegetables in a large Dutch oven and poured seasoned tomato sauce over them; then he covered them and set them to simmer on the back of the range. After preparing a salad and warming a fresh loaf of French bread, he set the table and poured the wine. His friend arrived just in time for dinner at five.

"Well, I couldn't wait to start dinner, so delicious was the aroma of Dwight's culinary masterpiece. To tell the truth, I wondered whether he had been entirely honest with me about how much he enjoyed my cooking. Never had I felt more of an amateur in the kitchen!

"However, when we all sat down at the beautifully set table with a floral centerpiece, I was truly honored that he wanted to cook for me. The salad was perfect, the bread hot and crusty, the wine perfectly chilled. Finally, when

Dwight brought his 'pièce de résistance' to the table, we applauded, so artfully had he arranged the platter. Each perfect orb was intact and resting in its assigned place on the platter, basking in a pool of garlicky tomato sauce. Dwight took a sharp knife and cut each vegetable in half, so we could each taste all of them.

"Then, it happened! As Dwight cut each vegetable apart, the two halves split apart revealing the stuffing. Only - the rice was raw! So precisely had Dwight fitted the tops on each veggie, that the simmering sauce had never found a way to get in to cook the stuffing. They had been hermetically sealed by the perfection of Dwight's technique.

"Of course, we made light of the situation, and made a good meal of bread, salad and whatever we could salvage of the main course. The Italian rum cake that Dwight had brought for dessert helped to save the day as well.

"Now, I must admit that secretly I was relieved. As I learned that day, sometimes there can be such a thing as 'too perfect'. The very same capabilities that make a good engineer may cause problems that no one expects in a non-engineering setting.

"On the other side of this human equation, Margo and Jerome Aguilar could not have been more different, We first met them when we were selling our house in Los Angeles so that we could move up here to Dos Hermanas. They answered our 'For Sale by Owner' ad in the local newspaper by calling and making an appointment to see the property.

"At exactly eleven o'clock on a Sunday morning, the doorbell chimed and when I opened the front door, there were two of the roundest people I ever saw. Margo was enormous. She was about five feet, four inches in height and as wide across as she was tall. She wore a brightly patterned muumuu and zori sandals. Her perfectly average size head sat on top of her rotund body like Humpty-Dumpty on a wall. Her brown hair was still wet from a shower and she had pulled it back tightly and twisted it into a small neat bun on the back of her head. A pair of friendly blue eyes twinkled in their nest of creases behind Margo's rimless spectacles. She smiled sweetly as I ushered them into our living room. Jerry was not much taller than his wife. A sparse thatch of silky brown hair, which he had parted on the side, topped his round ruddy face. Margo exuded an air of warmth and friendliness. She seemed to chatter on endlessly about one thing or another, with no particular connection to anything that was happening at the moment. Jerry, on the other hand was strictly business with no words wasted on trivia.

"I took them for a tour of our little house, mouthing the usual inane things one says in this situation: 'This is the kitchen; this is the master bedroom,' as though they might mistake the bathroom for the kitchen and wonder why we had a bath tub and commode there.

"When we returned to the living room, Jerry took a tape measure from his pocket and knelt down by the fireplace. As he measured the width, depth and height of the hearth, Ernie, my husband, asked him curiously what he was doing. Jerry answered that he was measuring the fireplace as though that were the most normal thing in the world.

"'I can see that, Jerry,' Ernie responded, 'but why?'

"Jerry paused for a moment and then explained that he was measuring the fireplace to see if it was large enough for their cauldron and spider.

"'Your what?' I asked, not comprehending.

Margo beat Jerry to the punch by supplying the answer before he could even begin.

"'A spider is the iron rack which supports our cauldron. A cauldron is a big iron kettle. The fireplace has to be big enough to hold them, so we can use them for our religious ceremonies…We're witches, you see,' she went on breezily, 'although we greatly prefer being called "Wiccans."'"

"'I thought witches were fictional creatures that come out on Halloween and ride around on broomsticks,' I interjected.

"'Oh, that's just silliness,' Margo replied, 'although I often like to say that I'm a very modern witch and I fly around on a vacuum cleaner. Actually, our religion is called "The Wicca" and we are called "Wiccans," which means "wise ones." Ours is probably the oldest living religion on earth. It is often called "The old religion" because it predates Christianity and Judaism by a thousand years or more.'

At this point, Jerry was through measuring and got to his feet, having decided that the fireplace was not quite big enough. I was intrigued by what Margo had told us, so I invited them to sit down with us for a cup of coffee. Little did I know that this would be the start of a friendship that introduced us to a whole different way of life.

Now, I hasten to add that although 'The Wicca' was fascinating to hear about, and Margo thought I'd make a great witch, neither Ernie nor I ever had the slightest inclination to join their 'coven,' which is what a congregation of thirteen witches is called.

"One evening, when Margo and Jerome came to our house for dinner, I asked Margo whether Wiccans could cast spells.

"'Yes, we can, but never to benefit ourselves, nor may we accept any form of payment. Our religion forbids it. It is also taboo to cast spells for any evil purpose; if we do, the evil will be turned against us.'

"'Do these spells actually work?' I persisted.

"Jerome spoke up: 'As a matter of fact, it is not well known by the public, but during World War II, when the allied forces were preparing for the Normandy invasion, the weather in the area turned very stormy and cold in the north Atlantic. The Allied High Command contacted the Wiccans of Great Britain and asked them to do what they could to bring on good weather. So, all of the Wiccans of Britain, Ireland and Wales met on the same night to cast a spell all together. When they were finished, the skies suddenly cleared and the storms abated long enough for the invasion to commence the landing of the allied troops on Omaha Beach. The rest, as they say, is history.'

"I had never heard this story, but Jerome assured me that it was well documented. As we got to know the Aguilars better, other inexplicable things surfaced.

"For example, Margo had what she called her 'familiar spirit,' named 'Ethan'. He had been a soldier during the American Revolution, or so she said. He could be found at the Aguilar house, although I never actually saw him. Margo confided that if she forgot to greet Ethan when she first came into the kitchen in the morning, he would rattle the dishes and bang on the pots and pans until she did. I suspected that Ethan might be a figment of Margo's lively imagination. However I soon learned not to dismiss Ethan so lightly.

"One evening, Ernie and I arranged to meet the Aguilars at a restaurant halfway between their house and ours. I drove my own car as Ernie was meeting us there straight from work. We had a very pleasant evening and finally, at about half past nine, we paid the check and prepared to go home. I was rather nervous about driving my big Ford station wagon home after dark on the freeway by myself. My night vision is not the greatest. After saying our 'Goodbyes,' I got into my car and started the motor. As I pulled out of the restaurant parking lot and onto the freeway ramp, I suddenly had a strange feeling that someone or something was sitting in the back seat, directly behind me. As I accelerated to sixty-five miles an hour, I could not turn to see what or who it was. I kept my eyes safely on the road, but as I drove, I sensed that whatever or whoever it was, it was a benign presence. I felt warmth emanating from behind me and I was able to drive the forty-five minutes without a problem. I left the freeway at the correct exit, and, without realizing what I was doing, I said 'Thank you' to my unseen companion for the comfort of his presence. At that point, he or she or it left me. I drove the rest of the way home by myself, along the familiar neighborhood streets.

"The next day, I called Margo. 'Was Ethan with you when you came to the restaurant last night,' I asked her. 'Yes, he was,' she replied.

"'Did he go home with you afterward?'

"Margo thought for a moment. 'No, as a matter of fact, he didn't.'

"'Am I crazy, or did Ethan ride home with me?'

"'Oh, no. You're perfectly sane,' she assured me, 'Ethan occasionally does things like that with friends of ours he especially likes.'

"Now, I can't prove that Ethan existed or did any of the things attributed to him. I only know what I felt. Those of you who know me well can testify that I usually have both of my feet firmly planted on the ground...But, I know what I know.'

"Well, be that as it may, the strangest event hadn't yet happened. It was a short time later that Dwight was hospitalized for surgery on a large kidney stone. The surgery was a success, but Dwight's incision was not healing properly. Indeed, it didn't seem to want to heal at all! The doctors refused to release Dwight from the hospital until it showed marked improvement. Ernie and I went to visit him and found him in a rather depressed state. 'Believe me,' said Dwight, 'if willpower could make it heal, I'd be back at work tomorrow. I'm bored silly just lying here like this.'

"That evening, as I was finishing up the dinner dishes, I had a call from Margo.

"'Luisa, I need a favor from you,' she announced after we had exchanged pleasantries. 'John Woodman, you know...the one who wrote all those books on ghosts and other psychic manifestations; well, anyway he's in town for a few days on a speaking tour. He's an old friend of ours and he's asked me to cast a spell to help one of his friends who is seriously ill. Well, you know how crowded our apartment is, what with all the kid junk, the cats and all.'

"Having visited their apartment, I knew exactly what she meant; I don't think they ever threw anything out!

"'Well,' Margo went on, 'I thought perhaps you wouldn't mind letting us do our healing ceremony at your house. It always looks so neat and tidy. It won't take long, maybe a half hour at most,' she assured me.

"'It sounds okay to me,' I told her, 'but let me just check with Ernie.' After conferring with him briefly, I told her it was okay. We settled on the following evening at eight o'clock for their ceremony.

"At eight o'clock sharp, Margo and Jerome materialized on our doorstep. A tall, distinguished looking gentleman was with them. They put me in mind of two sturdy tugboats towing an elegant ocean liner into port. I invited them in and after introductions had been attended to, Margo busied herself with preparations for the healing ceremony. I asked Margo if there was anything I could do to help.

"'Not really,' she replied, 'but you may watch my preparations if you like. It is forbidden for you and Ernie to be present at the actual ritual because you are not Wiccans. However, if you wish, I can include the name of anyone among your friends and family who may also be in need of healing. Just write the name on a piece of paper and give it to me,' Margo directed.

"So I wrote Dwight Singer's name on a slip of paper, with the information that he was in Cedars of Lebanon Hospital in Los Angeles.

"I watched as Margo took several skeins of embroidery thread out of a large tapestry tote bag. After cutting lengths of thread from several skeins—red, green, and purple—she laid them down carefully in a strange pattern on a square of white linen she had brought with her. She took several candles of the same colors and placed each one in a holder. Then she took the slip of paper with Dwight's name on it and placed it carefully between the threads and the candles. When she was done, she called Jerome and John Woodman to come over to the coffee table where she had arranged her little altar.

"I took Ernie by the arm and led him into the kitchen while I explained that we couldn't observe the ritual. I closed the door behind us, and poured us each a cup of tea. We sat at the kitchen table while the ceremony went on in the next room. I must admit that I hushed Ernie when he started to talk, and eavesdropped for all I was worth, but all I could hear was the murmur of voices.

"Ten minutes later, Margo came to tell us that the ritual was done. We rejoined the three of them in the living room and chatted a while longer. Then, at about nine o'clock, they left.

"The next morning, I called Dwight at the hospital. Ernie was just as curious as I was to find out if Margo's efforts had resulted in any improvement in Dwight's condition. I called the hospital number and got connected to Dwight's extension. The phone rang twice and then Dwight answered.

"'Hello, who's this?' he began. His voice sounded uncharacteristically guarded and cool.

"'It's Luisa,' I answered. 'Dwight, is anything wrong?'

"'Oh, Lu, it's you. Look, something very weird just happened and I've got to tell this to someone, but you've gotta promise you won't tell anyone else.'

"'Not even Ernie?' I asked.

"'Well, I guess Ernie's okay...he's pretty close mouthed.'

"I gestured to Ernie to pick up the phone in the kitchen. He moved quickly and picked up the phone to listen in. Dwight cleared his throat and began.

"'I got out of bed this morning at about seven-thirty and went into the bathroom to take a shower. I stepped into the shower stall and turned on the water, and I was just lathering up when I got this very strange feeling that I wasn't by myself. I mean I had a strong sense that there was someone or something in the shower with me.'

"'Male or female,' I asked.

"'Well, that's strange, too. It was definitely a male presence, and he was very tall at that...not that I could actually see anything clearly; it was pretty foggy.'

"'Who do you think it could be?' asked Ernie.

"'I have no idea, but whoever it was began to press firmly against my incision.'

"'Oh my God, did he hurt you?'

"'No, not at all, but it made me feel very nervous and jumpy, so I pushed him away from me...Then, he just disappeared,' said Dwight.

"Ernie and I were silent for a few moments while we digested what Dwight had told us. Then I told him all about Margo and her healing ritual for him.

"'I guess that the 'presence' you sensed was Ethan, Margo's spirit friend,' I told him. 'Maybe there really is something to all of the things that Margo has told us about the Wicca.'

"'Well,' said Dwight, 'this whole affair is too spooky for me. It goes against everything I know. What do you say that we keep this whole event among the three of us? People are going to think we're crazy if we tell them. If it didn't happen to me, I'd never believe it!' Ernie and I agreed.

"Within a day, Dwight's incision healed to the point where the doctors felt it safe to release him from the hospital. They were amazed at the quick turn-around in Dwight's condition. Ernie and I kept mum, even though we knew the truth. A promise is, after all a promise.

*   *   *   *   *   *   *   *   *

Well, we did eventually manage to sell our Los Angeles house to a young family from Iowa. Then, we came up here to Dos Hermanas, and as often happens in our mobile society, we lost track of Margo and Jerome when they moved out of state. Dwight changed jobs and moved to be closer to his work. He did not leave a forwarding address.

"Just last year, we received an invitation in the mail from one of Ernie's former co-workers in Los Angeles. It was quite a surprise, seeing as how we've been away from there for over twenty years, and have made a good life for ourselves right here in Dos Hermanas.

"Ernie and I talked it over and decided it would be fun to renew old acquaintances. So we drove down to Los Angeles, and stayed at a local hotel for a long weekend.

"The reunion was scheduled for Saturday evening, starting at five o'clock. We arrived at Petrelli's Steak House, which was close to the original site of the factory where they had all worked. We arrived there about five-thirty and there were already a number of old timers chatting, drinking beer or wine, and raising a cheerful hubbub with their voices. When we walked in, we got a rousing welcome from all and sundry.

"Ernie recognized most of the people he'd worked with, even though many had put on a few pounds and gone gray. Some of the people we remembered, however, had not been able to come because of other commitments. I looked around from face to face and finally saw Dwight Singer standing near the bar with a pretty younger woman.

"I worked my way through the crowd and was warmly greeted by Dwight, who introduced me to the young woman,

"'Darling, I'd like you to meet an old friend of mine. Luisa, this is my wife, Laurie.' I smiled at her and extended my hand for a handshake.

"'You must be very special, Laurie. Ernie and I always thought that Dwight was a confirmed bachelor. How wonderful that he found you!'

"'Oh, I guess I'm the lucky one,' she answered sweetly. 'We couldn't be happier.'

"'And how about you, you old rascal,' teased Ernie,

"'Where did you find this sweet young thing? In high school?'

"Dwight laughed, and Laurie smiled and came to his defense:

"'Oh, I'm not as young as all that. Don't let my blonde hair fool you; if it weren't for a great hair dresser, I'd have almost as many gray hairs as Dwight does.'

"I rather doubted that, but admired Laurie's concern for Dwight's feelings. Of course, he was not the least bit offended by Ernie. Dwight playfully cuffed Ernie's ear, and turned to his wife.

"'Honey, don't you take a word this man says as serious. I never have.'

Just then, we were all called into the next room to begin dinner. Ernie and I sat with Dwight and Laurie and continued to rehash old times.

"After we'd finished dessert and had poured a second cup of coffee from the carafe on the table, Laurie excused herself for 'a trip to the little girl's room.' When she was well out of earshot, Ernie asked Dwight,

"'Have you had any more problems with your kidney, Dwight? I remember you had quite a difficult time for a while there.'

"'Well, yeah, I was pretty sick back then, but I started to become much more health conscious and, knock wood, I've been pretty much okay since then.' He rapped his knuckles on the table to emphasize his point.

"'That's good to hear,' I commented. 'I still remember how shaken you were when our Wiccan friend cast a spell to help you heal. Have you had any more visits from Ethan?'

"Dwight looked at me uncomprehendingly.

"'I'm sorry, Lu, I have no idea what you're talking about. Who's Ethan? Are you sure it's not someone else you're thinking of?'

"'Surely, you can't have forgotten, Dwight,' interjected Ernie, but I quickly put my hand on his arm and gave it a squeeze under the table.

"'Perhaps you're right,' I said, 'It must have been someone else.'

"Ernie gave me a strange look, but he took the hint and said no more. Anyway, Laurie returned to our table at that point and I didn't think she'd be able to deal with the reality of what happened so many years ago. Clearly, Dwight wasn't able to, either! So I shrugged and decided it was best not to say any more about it.

"When Ernie and I were once again alone in our car, we felt free to talk about what had happened.

"'I can't believe he doesn't remember,' I commented.

"'Oh, I can, Lu. When someone like Dwight encounters something outside his concept of reality, sometimes the only way he can deal with it is to deny, even to himself, that it ever happened. You and I are the only ones who know the truth.'

"'Yes, I guess that's true…I never would have guessed that a witch would be more reality based than an engineer, would you?' I commented. Ernie smiled and said.

"'Nope.'

*   *   *   *   *   *   *   *   *

"It's been many years since it all happened, and we haven't seen Dwight, or Margo and Jerry since. You, dear friends and former patients, are the very first people to whom I have entrusted this story. Now, you may choose to believe my story or not. It's all the same to Ernie and me…But, as I've often said before, 'I know what I know!'"

Luisa smiled and inclined her head to indicate the end of her story. At first, there was silence as her audience let her tale sink in; but then, they started to clap vigorously and whistle and cheer. Luisa bowed to all and rejoined her husband at their table.

CHAPTER NINE

In the book of Genesis, there is a remarkable story about Creation. In seven days, it is said, God created heaven and earth. Now it came to pass that the first man and his mate were allowed to dwell in a garden paradise called "Eden." All their needs were provided for, and there was nothing to mar their joy in each other and their idyllic home, until the serpent arrived on the scene and ruined everything. Why did God create the serpent?

The Storysmith

* * * * * * * * *

Tuesday morning was there almost before Miranda knew it. "I don't know where Monday disappeared to," she grumbled.

"Yeah, I know what you mean, Miranda," sympathized Danny. "It feels like just last night that Ms. Marino told her story. I mean, I know it was really on Sunday evening, but I couldn't stop wondering about it all day yesterday."

"Really? What did you think about Ms. Marino's story?" asked Miranda.

Danny considered her question for a few moments.

"I'm not sure what I think, Miranda," he answered.

"I mean it was a pretty far out story, wasn't it? You know, with witches and ghosts and all that stuff...I never believed in the supernatural very much...until now, at least. But she made it sound so real, that I don't know what to believe."

"I guess that's what a really good story teller does," Miranda answered.

"She gets her listeners to suspend their reality for a little while just to make the story better."

"Do you mean you don't think it's true?" asked Danny.

"Oh, I didn't say that," she replied. "Maybe Luisa's story is true, or maybe not. Only she knows for sure, but I think each person creates his or her own reality."

"Wow, that's heavy, Miranda. What do you mean? Like we all see everything differently? Or like some people see ghosts and witches and the rest of us don't?"

"I don't think it's all that dramatic, Danny. On things that are readily observable and measurable, most people would agree; for example, you and I both agree that this is my coffee cup. But that doesn't mean we see it exactly alike. My color spectrum may be different from yours, so I may see it as baby blue, while you see it as aqua or lavender. What we usually think of as a shared reality is really consensus. We have agreed that these are coffee cups of a color we have agreed to call blue. Do you get what I mean?"

Danny thought it over.

"I think so. So, maybe Ms. Marino's reality includes witches and all that, but mine doesn't. So who's right?"

"It isn't a question of right and wrong, Danny. It's a question of what we agree to believe."

"What do you believe, Miranda? Are there witches and ghosts and things?"

"It all depends, Danny. I know for certain that there are people who call themselves 'Witches' or 'Wiccans'. I've met some."

"Do they cast spells and meet with Satan and all that?" asked Danny.

"The Wiccans I know have nothing to do with the devil; that's Satanism and it is bent on doing evil and creating mischief. 'The Wicca' is a very old religion based on the workings of Mother Nature, or 'Gaia,' as she is sometimes called. They are forbidden to use their powers for bad purposes; if they do, the evil turns back on them. They do have their own liturgy, just as Judaism and Christianity do, and when they pray, they may do it differently from others, but the intent is the same."

"When you explain it that way, it seems perfectly reasonable, Miranda, but how about the spirit world? Do you think there are spirits like in Ms. Merino's story?"

"I'm certainly willing to allow for that possibility. There are a lot of things that go on in this world for which we have no rational explanation. Until we do, I suppose spirits are as good an explanation as any. Think about it, Danny; before we knew anything about germs, evil spirits or 'bad humours' were blamed for the spread of disease. I think we're just at the beginning of understanding our universe, including the spirit world, or heaven and hell, if they exist."

"Yeah, I can see your point, Miranda…You sure do know a lot about Wiccans, don't you? I have to ask…Miranda, are you a Wiccan?"

Miranda smiled, "If by that, you mean do I belong to the organized religion called 'The Wicca,' my answer is 'No.'"

*   *   *   *   *   *   *   *   *

Tanya paused outside the Dos Hermanas Hospital and checked her watch. It was exactly eleven forty-five.

"Damn," she said aloud, although she was quite alone. "Fifteen minutes to wait in this boring one-horse town. What a drag."

She sat down on the steps and leaned back against the side railing. Then she reached into her purse and pulled out a package of "Virginia Slims." She fished around some more in the large black leather pouch and finally felt the coolness of her cigarette lighter. She pulled it out and flicked the wheel of the lighter a few times. It wouldn't light, so Tanya tossed it carelessly over her shoulder into the bushes behind the railing. Muttering to herself, she finally located a book of matches and lit her cigarette. Gratefully, she sucked in a deep breath of smoke and then allowed it to escape through her nostrils.

"You've come a long way, Babe," she hummed the 'Virginia Slims' jingle softly to herself. Well, maybe I haven't come a long way yet," she mused, "but just wait!

"If this works out the way I think it will, this could be the start of my whole career as a journalist. Watch out world, here I come!" She grinned and took another drag on her cigarette. She checked her wristwatch one more time and then, she turned her attention to the story Luisa Marino had told at the cafe.

"What if there really are witches here in Dos Hermanas? That ought to create a stir! Just think of it...a coven of witches having secret meetings, with weird rituals and evil spells, dancing around a cauldron in the buff. Man, I bet all hell would break loose! And what a hot story I could write. The big city papers would get hold of it and I could get hired as a reporter for a REAL newspaper, instead of this two bit small town rag."

Miranda's Muse

On Monday after the story telling session at Miranda's Cafe, Tanya had phoned Luisa and made an appointment for lunch today. She told Luisa that she was writing an article about the contest for the Fort Bragg Newspaper and that she was interviewing all the entrants. Tanya thought it would be better not to mention "The Braggart" by name. It wasn't exactly prestigious like "The Fort Bragg Sentinel" was.

Just then, Tanya spotted Luisa in her nurse's uniform coming out through the revolving door of the hospital. She got to her feet and went up the steps.

"Mrs. Merino? I'm Tanya McCullough. Thanks for coming. I'm really interested in your story about the witch. I'm dying to find out whether all that actually happened the way you say it did in your story".

Luisa smiled and said: "I've had a lot of people ask me that. I haven't answered that question yet. Some things are better left ambiguous. Anyway, whatever I say, half the people who ask are going to believe me and the other half won't. So what's the point?" Luisa laughed and shook her head.

Tanya smiled and seemed to agree with Luisa. "Is there any other place but Miranda's Cafe in town where we could get lunch?" she asked. "It's such a social place, I'm afraid we'd be interrupted by all the people who know you there."

"Actually," Tanya thought to herself, "I'd rather Miranda didn't hear the questions I'm going to ask. She might not like them, and for sure, she'd call my mother and tell her about it, and then who knows what Mom might do?"

Luisa thought for a few seconds,

"The only other convenient place I can think of is the 'Denny's' just off the freeway ramp. I don't think we'd be interrupted. It's mostly tourists and travelers who stop there."

"Great! Let's go."

The two women climbed into the front seat of Tanya's black VW and drove off.

*   *   *   *   *   *   *   *   *

When Lucille Lorman came home from work on Thursday, she stopped, as usual, to pick up her mail. After sorting through it briefly, she tucked it into the outside pocket of her large brown leather shoulder bag. She was just about to unlock the front door to her apartment, when she noticed that the local evening paper, with its accompaniment of throwaways, junk mail, and "The Pennysaver" were waiting for her in an untidy heap by her front door. She picked them up and let herself in before glancing through them. On most Thursdays, she didn't bother to look at them, but she had placed an ad in "The Pennysaver" for a couple of lamps she wanted to sell and thought she'd make sure it was printed correctly.

As she sorted through the pile, "The Braggart" caught her eye, something about Dos Hermanas. She took it with her into the kitchen and sat down at the table to check it out. She read the headline out loud:

"Dos Hermanas Nurse Admits to Consorting With Witches! Story on Page Two."

Lucille turned quickly to page two and continued to read:

"Luisa Marino doesn't look like the kind of person who consorts with witches, but the story she told on Sunday evening at Miranda's Cafe, a popular hangout for locals in

Dos Hermanas, sounded a little too realistic to have been made up out of whole cloth. When this reporter interviewed Ms Marino, a registered nurse at Dos Hermanas Hospital, Nurse Marino stated '…it's true, although I don't expect most people will believe it.' She said that although she had changed the names of the witch and warlock in her story, most of the facts were correct, including the fact that the witches in question conducted secret rites in her home and that they had used secret spells on hospitalized patients. This reporter wonders if the hospital administration was aware of this when Nurse Marino was hired. Perhaps someone should check whether anything strange has occurred since she took over."

The article ended with the by line, 'Tanya McCullough.'

Lucille put the newspaper down on the kitchen table with a slam.

"What a rotten thing to say about Luisa Marino! My God, what is this world coming to, when a good person like her can be attacked in the local papers by such a vicious liar? Who is this Tanya McCullough person, anyhow?"

She shook her head in disbelief, picked up the telephone and dialed.

"Miranda? This is Lucille. Have you seen today's 'Braggart' yet?"

"Oh, hi Lucille. No, I can't say I have. Why? What's the matter? You sound upset."

"I am upset, Miranda. Do you have a copy there, or should I bring one over?"

"I usually just put it in the trash, but maybe I can rescue it. What's wrong?"

"Miranda, I'm so mad, I could spit fire! You will be too when you see what it says about Luisa Marino and her entry in the story contest."

"Okay, Lucy. Let see if I can lay my hands on 'The Braggart,' so I'll know what you're talking about. I'll call you back after I've read it."

Miranda placed the receiver back in the cradle and went over to the trashcan. After a few minutes of searching, she found what she was looking for. She placed the paper on the table and stared at the headline.

"I don't believe it," she remarked aloud. "What has that foolish child done? The editor who let this go through must be off his rocker! Why there's not a true word in it. I'd better call Luisa right now and warn her. I hope she hasn't seen this yet!"

Miranda called Dos Hermanas Hospital and asked whether Luisa Marino was on duty this evening. The hospital operator informed her that she was, but that she had asked not to be disturbed by any more telephone calls, except for emergencies. Miranda thanked her and hung up.

"I guess I am not the first one to call,' she remarked. "I'll try her at home in the morning." She checked her watch and went into the kitchen to finish her day's work so she could lock up and go home.

* * * * * * * * *

As Miranda drove, her mind was racing. As a wild tumble of "what ifs" and "maybe I shoulds" rolled helter-skelter through her thoughts, she realized that her foot was keeping rhythm with her mind. She was alternately speeding and then catching herself and slowing down.

"Not a good way to drive, Miranda," she chided herself, "You'd better pull over and think this through."

She waited until she reached the roadside clearing she had come to think of as her own and sat quietly for a few minutes. Then she got out and walked to the edge of the clearing. The moon was not full tonight, but there was still enough of her silver light to reflect off the treetops and the silent hills. Miranda took a deep breath and let the fragrant night air work it's magic.

She counted from ten to one and allowed all connected thought to fly away from her. As she reached the last number, a cloud covered the moon and Miranda felt a chilly darkness falling over her. Rather than the sense of serenity she expected, she was overwhelmed by a sense of foreboding. She drew her breath in sharply and looked around her.

An automobile was pulling off the highway behind Miranda's pickup truck. She started toward the Toyota, remembering that she had left her keys in the ignition. Before she could get around to the driver's side, however, someone jumped out of the passenger side of the automobile, and came toward her.

"Hey, lady, how far to the nearest gas station?" A young man came toward her. She could see a hank of greasy blonde hair and the glowing end of a cigarette hanging loosely out of his mouth. The smell of it blotted out the sweet smell of the night air.

Miranda pointed in the direction from which she had come.

"It's just a couple of miles that way," she replied, and continued to edge slowly toward her truck.

She was startled to find that the driver of the other vehicle had come around the driver side of the Toyota and was standing there waiting for her.

"Ain't no use finding a gas station, Jocko," he called to his companion, "We ain't got but a buck between us."

Miranda could feel her body tightening up as she realized how vulnerable she was here. No one would hear her if there was trouble. She had never been afraid to go anywhere alone before, especially not here.

"The world has become a very different place from what it used to be," she thought, "There is danger now that never was there before. Oh, my Goddess, if ever I needed help, I think it's now!"

She forced herself to remain calm, or at least outwardly controlled.

"I guess I've got a few dollars I could let you have for gas," she offered. "It's tough to be stuck someplace without money, and I imagine you dudes are in a hurry."

The driver laughed in a very unpleasant way. Miranda could see his shaved head clearly now and a straggly growth of beard on his gaunt face.

"Oh yeah, Granny, I just bet you've got a few bucks in that pick-up all right."

He pulled the door open, reached in and took her purse from its place on the seat.

"Never mind, Granny, I'll save you the trouble," he sneered.

He opened her purse and pulled out her wallet. Opening it roughly, he took out all the money she had and threw the wallet and the purse at her feet. Suddenly, Miranda could feel her anger rising like a white-hot tide. She pulled herself up tall.

"Well," she said indignantly, "I guess your mother would just love to see what you've become, you bully! Robbing old ladies of their last penny! Aren't you the big brave hero! Why don't you pick on someone your own size?"

He stepped back involuntarily at the fury of her onslaught. Then he regained the swaggering bravado he'd begun with.

"Oh shut your face, you old bitch, before I shut you up for good!"

As he started toward her, Miranda could see the other thug coming around the front of the Toyota. She looked around for an escape route, but there was no place she could run without encountering one of her attackers. She froze in place. As he came menacingly toward her, she could hear a rustling in the bushes. Suddenly there was a loud sinister growl.

The moon reappeared and then, Miranda saw her! It was the old she-wolf, but she was not the friendly canine who had howled at the moon with Miranda. Her golden eyes were blazing with an unholy light and her formidable teeth were bared menacingly. The thick gray hair at the back of her neck was standing upright and bristling. She growled again and came toward them, picking up speed as she moved. Her lips were drawn back from her fangs and she was slavering, the frothy saliva dripping from her jaws.

The two thugs turned on their heels and ran for their car, screaming in fear. The wolf followed them closely, nipping at their heels and snapping at their ankles. As they threw themselves into their car, the wolf leapt easily onto the hood and continued to menace them through the windshield. They started the motor and lurched back onto the highway.

The old she-wolf slipped off the hood and stood watching them careen from one side of the road to the other as they made their escape. Then she turned back toward Miranda and casually trotted to her.

Miranda sat down heavily on the gravelly dirt and tried to catch her breath. Finally, she was able to speak without panting.

"My dear, this is the second time I've had reason to be grateful for your presence. Thank you for coming to my rescue."

Ever so slowly, she raised her hand to stroke the wolf's head and haunches. The wolf sat quietly and allowed Miranda's gentle gesture.

"I love you, Sister Wolf," she said simply.

* * * * * * * * *

Neither Miranda nor the she wolf had noticed the third person sitting in the back of the automobile now careening wildly down the highway. But Tanya had watched the whole episode intently. Now, she screamed at her companions:

"For Christ's sake, you idiots, slow down before you kill us all!"

* * * * * * * * *

It was very late when Tanya got back to her apartment in Fort Bragg. After emptying her mailbox, she climbed the stairs and unlocked her apartment door. She turned on the lights, got a Coke from the refrigerator and plunked herself down on the sofa to think.

"I wonder if Miranda called the cops when she got home. It's a good thing she didn't see me, because I'd really be in hot water if she knew I had anything to do with it."

She sat a while longer, sipping at her drink and idly tapping on the arm of the sofa with her fingernails.

"Well, maybe I can work something out, so that I get a good story out of it anyway," she thought. "Like what, Tanya?" she asked herself.

Suddenly, she sat bolt upright and started to laugh out loud.

"I've got it! I'm going to get an even better story out of this! I'll beat Miranda to the punch!"

Tanya reached for the phone and hastily dialed the number of the friends she had just left.

"Listen, guys, this is Tanya and I've got a great idea. Just do what I tell you and I'll explain later. Okay? Great!"

CHAPTER TEN

Chaim Yankel had a problem with God. "God," he prayed, "If you don't mind my asking, why do you make life so hard for us Jews? I have to work ten hours a day just to get enough to feed my children. You make my poor wife go through terrible pain every time she gives birth. The anti-Semites make us suffer just for being Jews. Couldn't you have made life a little easier?"

God heard Chaim Yankel's plea and had compassion. "Chaim Yankel," He called, "I hear you. Your complaint is not unjust, but it is too late for me the change the whole world for you. However I have decided to give you a wonderful gift which will help you to cope with your problems."

Chaim Yankel couldn't wait to hear what God's gift would be. "Thank you, God, but what is this gift?"

"Chaim Yankel, the special gift I have for you and your brethren is called 'Laughter.'"

And Chaim Yankel laughed.

The Storysmith

* * * * * * * * *

Miranda and Irene were just finishing up the last minute preparations for tonight's fourth dinner and story presentation. Melanie and Danny were in the dining room, completing the table setting with flower vases on each table. Miranda had decided to splurge and provide fresh roses of different colors for the bud vases. Each table had one rose and a sprig of fresh rosemary from the herb garden. The combination of sweet and spicy scents pleased Miranda.

Melanie had suggested using small gold paper doilies under each vase and the effect was to make the cafe look even more festive than usual.

"That was a good idea, Melanie," Miranda commented. "You certainly do have an eye for decorating."

Melanie nodded and responded softly: "I'm glad you like it, Miranda."

As Miranda returned to the kitchen, the back door of the cafe opened suddenly and Ruthie limped in and waved her cane as though it was a magic wand.

"Greetings, one and all. It's me, Ruthie…And it won't be long before I'm ready to come back to work. This lazy life is not for the likes of Ruth O'Brien!"

Although she still needed her cane for balance, Ruthie looked great.

"Welcome back, Ruthie," said Miranda." It's good to see you looking so well. You must be getting a lot of rest."

Irene wiped her hands on a paper towel and came forward to greet Ruthie.

"I'm glad to see you're healing, Ruthie; I've been helping Miranda while you're recuperating."

"And the saints bless you for doing it, Irene," replied Ruthie. "The doctor says I'll be able to come back part time in just a few weeks, as long as I'm not on my feet for too long at a stretch. So don't be running away yet, my dear."

Just then, Danny came through the swinging doors from the dining room.

"I thought I heard a familiar voice," he said smiling broadly.

Then he made his way around the kitchen table and gave Ruthie a big hug and a loud kiss on the cheek.

"Aah, I've got you in me clutches now, me proud beauty and for once you can't get away," he teased.

"Well, to tell the truth, Danny, I'm not wantin' to run away—it's that good to see you!"

The door swung open again and this time it was Melanie who joined the group in the kitchen. She welcomed Ruthie with a smile and a hug. Ruthie returned her embrace, and then held Melanie out at arm's length for a better view of her.

"It does my heart good to see you, child. Look at you—you're prettier than ever!"

Melanie colored ever so slightly and dipped her head in acknowledgment. Ruthie turned back to Miranda.

"I was thinking of coming in for half a day on Tuesday if that's convenient for you, Miranda…You know, just to try me legs out."

"That'll be great, Ruthie. Irene and I will both be here, so we can be your legs if you need us."

"Don't be spoiling me too much now," laughed Ruthie.

"Don't worry yourself, Ruthie. I don't think we will coddle you any more than you want us to…Now, is Clyde waiting for you outside?"

Ruth nodded affirmatively.

"Well, let's not all stand around gabbing then. Danny, please find places for Ruthie and Clyde in the dining room. Tonight, they are our honored guests."

"That's an offer I can't refuse," laughed Ruthie.

Miranda's Muse

After Ruthie and Clyde had been seated, dinner was served. Tonight's main course was Hungarian goulash, with spicy paprika gravy enriched with a generous helping of sour cream just before serving. The wide poppy seeded egg noodles that accompanied the goulash made an attractive base for the meat and gravy, especially after Irene sprinkled fresh chopped parsley over the top. Steamed baby carrots completed the main course. Later, a delicious home made apple strudel served with bowls of fresh whipped cream and accompanied by fresh brewed strong coffee would complete the meal.

As Miranda checked to see that everyone had been served, she noticed that some people were missing from the audience. Luisa Marino and her husband were not present, nor was Tanya McCullough.

"Well, I'm not surprised that the little brat isn't here, after the ridiculous things she wrote. She should be ashamed of herself!" thought Miranda.

She felt uneasy at the Marinos' absence. She resolved to call them as soon as possible to make sure they were okay.

When the dishes had been cleared and coffee and tea served, Miranda stepped up to the microphone.

"Welcome friends to the fourth and last story in our contest. After you rate tonight's presentation on the rating sheet we'll be handing out, we will tabulate the results of all four story evenings and come up with the name of the winner. Next Sunday, all of you who have participated in hearing and rating each story, as well as our four finalists and their families, are invited to be here at two in the afternoon for coffee and pie on the house. At that time, we will announce the winner of our first annual story contest and award prizes to the winner and the runners-up."

There was a burst of applause and a few cheers and whistles from the audience. Miranda smiled at their enthusiasm and raised both hands for silence. Some of the diners shushed the others loudly, while others held index fingers to their lips to quiet the shushers. Finally, when everyone had quieted down, Miranda began the evening's program.

"Ladies and gentlemen, I am pleased to present our fourth and final story teller, Joshua Roberts. Let's welcome him."

As the applause subsided, a sturdily built young man with thinning golden brown hair strode purposefully up to the microphone. He looked comfortable in carefully pressed chino trousers and a colorful long sleeved plaid shirt. His brown leather loafers were polished to a high shine. Indeed, Josh looked as if he'd been polished and shined from head to toe. He adjusted his gold-rimmed spectacles, made himself comfortable on the storyteller's stool and smiled broadly at his audience.

"Good evening, folks," he addressed the crowd casually. "How're ya all doing?"

The crowd answered him in a similarly informal manner: "Fine, Josh"…"Okay"…"Great!" Then they settled back expectantly and waited for Josh to begin.

"I call my story, 'The Shtick.' It began when I was twelve years old and my mother decided to allow me to come along on a car trip to Montreal, Canada. We were going to pick up my big sister who was attending university there and bring her and her stuff home for the summer. We started out on a beautiful spring day. My Aunt Betty, who was my mom's older sister, had agreed to come along to help with the driving.

"Now, Mom and Aunt Betty were usually reasonable, calm and down to earth women. They'd worked hard raising their families. After we were all in school, they went back to teaching, but when their districts closed schools on account of a declining school population, both Mom and Aunt Betty changed careers. Mom became a counselor at a local community college and Aunt Betty opened a children's consignment shop.

"There was, however, one thing about them which might be considered unusual: When they were little girls, they had invented a game which they named 'Pretend.' They would concoct elaborate fantasies and then each would take a role and act it out, sometimes for days on end, according to my grandmother.

"Well, it seems as though they hadn't outgrown 'the game' as they now called it. If a situation arose which either of them deemed appropriate for a bit of role playing, Mom and Aunt Betty would, without a word or a warning, start to do 'a shtick.' In theater talk, 'a shtick' is a piece of theatrical business: something actors might use as part of a characterization or role.

"Anyway, as I sat quietly in the back seat of the car and watched the small towns and tree covered hillsides of northern New York State whiz by, my aunt drove our large green Ford Torino up the New York State Thruway and onto The Northway,' the most scenic highway in the United States,' according to the road signs we passed every so often.

"The speedometer read seventy two miles per hour as we passed the state trooper's car parked at the ready in a rest area on our right side. Aunt Betty remarked casually to my mother, 'Abby, it hardly pays to slow down. That cop has us on his radar for sure.'

"Aunt Betty was right. About two minutes later the flashing red lights on the trooper's car caught up with us. We slowed down and turned off the road onto a flat roadside viewpoint, where we stopped. As the black and white police car pulled up behind us, Aunt Betty fished around the front seat for her purse, opened the car door and jumped out onto the gravelly dirt. As she turned to her left and bounced over toward the police officer, I had a hunch that she was about to begin a shtick. Perhaps it was the way she waggled her denim clad behind as she made her way to where the officer stood, already filling out a ticket in his book that gave me the clue. I couldn't see how this particular shtick would evolve, but I settled down to watch, while Mom remained on the alert to be ready for her part in the little drama which was unfolding in front of us.

"Aunt Betty smiled her most engaging smile and ran her hand through her flowing salt-and-pepper hair.

"'Why, officer,' she gushed - and Aunt Betty never gushed when she was just being herself - 'this is such a gorgeous road and such a beautiful day…not another car on the road anywhere, except for yours, of course, that before I even knew it, there we were speeding along. I said to my sister, 'Abby', I said, 'Abby, I do believe that we are going to be stopped by that policeman.'"

"'Yes, Ma'am,' said the trooper. 'Do you know you were going over seventy miles per hour?'"

"'My goodness-gracious, that fast? Well, I guess Abby and I and my little nephew here were so busy talking and enjoying your beautiful scenery, that we just weren't paying attention to our speedometer the way we should.'"

"'Yes, Ma'am, I know that's easy to do.' he replied sympathetically.

"He stood there in his tall, shiny, black, knee high boots and smart looking uniform, neatly pressed into precise creases, with his ticket book and pen in hand. He was young, probably not more than twenty-three years old. His cheeks were smooth and rosy, and he had a carefully cultivated, small, neat black mustache, probably so he would look older and more serious; but his solemn dark eyes shown with good health and good humor. In a cutaway coat and an ascot tie, he'd have looked right at home on top of a wedding cake.

"At this point, my mother opened her car door and came around the back of our Ford. As she walked over toward her sister, the patrolman said politely to Aunt Betty: 'May I see your license, Ma'am?'

"Aunt Betty turned suddenly toward my mother. 'Abby, do you remember that time when your daughter had that fender-bender in my van? Well, I got the points for that on my license. How about taking them on your license this time?'

"Mom pondered the question momentarily.

"'That only seems fair, Sis. Okay.'

"She reached into her bag and pulled out her driver's license.

"'Here, officer," she said, as she handed him her license. 'Give me the ticket instead.'

"The young officer shifted uncertainly from one foot to the other. 'Well, Ma'am, I'm not sure I'm allowed to do that.'

"'Oh well,' babbled Mother cheerfully. 'What's the difference who gets the ticket as long as someone does?

After all, I'm just as much at fault as my sister is. I was sitting right there beside her, distracting her with my chatter. I should have noticed that we were speeding and said something about it.'

"'Uh, well, that is...er, May I see your vehicle registration, Ma'am?'

"Mom suddenly remembered that they were driving Dad's car because it had a bigger trunk, and she had forgotten to ask Dad for the car registration. She turned and went back to the passenger side of the Ford, opened the door and slid into the seat. Then she snapped open the glove box and started shuffling through the tightly packed stack of road maps, tour books, old receipts, tire guarantees and other oddly assorted junk that Dad always seemed to accumulate in his car.

"'I know it's here someplace,' she said, her voice rising nervously. 'I saw it here just the other day...I know,' she chattered shrilly. 'It must be in the trunk!'

As Mom leapt out of the front seat onto the gravel, Aunt Betty came rushing around the side of the car, followed by the trooper.

"'Now, Abby dear, take it easy and don't get yourself all in a tizzy; you know what the doctor said...You're not to get upset...We don't want you to have another attack, now do we?'

"My mother had never had an attack of anything worse than hives caused by an allergy to walnuts. Other than that, she was in perfect health. Truly, Aunt Betty had come up with a stroke of genius, no pun intended.

"The young officer was visibly worried now. That's all he would need on his so far unblemished record...that he had caused a sweet old lady, old enough to be his mother, for God's sake, to have 'an attack.' whatever that might be.

"'Never mind,' he said soothingly,

"'I see you have a current inspection sticker in your car window. That means the car is legally registered.' He dropped his hands to his sides, the ticket book in one hand, and the pen in the other. With a deep sigh, he turned toward Aunt Betty and asked her: 'Ma'am, do you think you could drive at something less than seventy miles per hour?'

"A long pause ensued as Aunt Betty cocked her head to one side, placed her left hand under her chin and thought about his question.

"'Well, officer, you're such a nice young man that I'd feel terrible if I told you a falsehood…No, I don't think I could drive under seventy. Even if I tried my very best, I am sure I would end up at least seventy on this road.'

The officer stood as if he'd been hit by lightening. Then, wearily, he turned toward my mother.

"'Ma'am.' he began again, 'do you think YOU could drive at less than seventy miles per hour?'

"'What speed do you have in mind?' she asked, clearly willing to negotiate her terms.

"'Well, Ma'am, how about sixty-five?'

"'Oh, that's only five miles an hour slower,' she bubbled happily. 'Yes, sir, I think I could manage that,' she conceded graciously.

"'Okay then, ladies, I'll let you go with just a warning if you'll keep your speed at less than sixty-six miles per hour. Please drive carefully,' he cautioned as he put his pen and ticket book back into his pocket.

"'Officer, you are just the best mannered, nicest young officer we've ever had the privilege of meeting,' enthused Aunt Betty, 'Your mother should be very proud of you!'

"'Yes, Ma'am. Thank you Ma'am.' he acknowledged and turned to go back to his car.

"Aunt Betty handed the keys to my mother and they got back into the Ford. Mom was in the driver's seat this time. She started the engine and waved merrily to the patrolman. He stood there, feet apart, and waved back. Then he turned slowly and shaking his head from side to side, got behind the wheel and turned toward the police barracks.

"We drove about five miles further north and then pulled off to the side of the road. Without a word having passed between them, both front doors flew open and Mom and Aunt Betty jumped, as sprightly as ever, onto the gravel shoulder. As Aunt Betty ran around the front of the car and Mom ran around the back of the car, they raised their arms and flapped their hands wildly shouting gibberish intended to sound like rapid Chinese. It was a classic 'Chinese fire drill' such as high school kids would stage occasionally when they were stopped at a long red light. As they slid back into the Ford, my aunt once again in the driver's seat, they turned toward each other with broad grins. After a simultaneous 'thumbs up,' we continued on our way to Montreal. It was clear to me that 'The Shtick' was complete."

The audience burst into delighted laughter and applause. Josh stood and took a small bow. He made his way back to the table where his wife and two daughters awaited him with hugs and kisses.

Miranda's Muse

"Josh," called out Fire Chief McCarthy, "Did that young New York Highway Patrolman have anything to do with your becoming a California Highway Patrolman?"

Josh looked up and grinned,

"Not a thing," he replied amiably, "but if I ever pull you over for speeding, Chief McCarthy, I wouldn't try a shtick if I were you."

*   *   *   *   *   *   *   *   *

Miranda waited until her crew had cleared the dining room, and were ready to leave.

"Before you go home, I'd like to say a most heartfelt 'Thank you' to each of you for helping to make this evening and all the other events connected with this contest so pleasant for everyone concerned: the patrons, the contestants, and especially for me. I couldn't have managed without each of you. You are wonderful and I am truly blessed by your friendship and support."

At first they were silent, and then Danny stepped forward.

"Miranda, I think I speak for all of us when I say 'Thank you' right back. I wouldn't have traded this experience for anything!"

Irene, Melanie and Ruthie, who had stayed after the patrons had left, nodded their agreement and gathered around Miranda with hugs and kisses for her and each other. Miranda saw them all out to the parking lot and waved to them as they drove off. Danny was the last to leave, and he gave her three short toots on his horn before he turned onto the street.

After checking around to make sure everything was ship-shape, Miranda locked the doors and turned the "Open" sign around so that "Closed" appeared in the cafe window. Then she looked up the phone number of Luisa Marino in her card file.

"It's only nine o'clock," she thought, "It's not too late to call and see if everything's okay."

She dialed the number and waited for the phone to ring at the other end. It rang several times before Luisa answered.

"Hello? This is Luisa. Who's calling, please?"

"Luisa, it's Miranda. Is everything all right? I've been trying to reach you, but I keep getting a busy signal. When you didn't show up tonight, I started to worry. What's happening?"

"Thanks, Miranda. I can understand your concern. We're both okay, but ever since that article came out in 'The Braggart,' all hell's been breaking loose."

"What do you mean?" asked Miranda. "Don't tell me that anyone has taken that ridiculous article seriously, Luisa."

"I know it's hard to believe, Miranda, but evidently there are people who will believe just about anything…and the way that Tanya McCullough wrote it, it sounded awful…as though I would ever do anything to harm a patient."

"Of course you wouldn't. Anyone who knows you knows that, Luisa."

"Until this happened, I'd have said the same, Miranda, but the way that wicked girl twisted my words, it sounds terrible! That's what's so insidious about what she did. She quoted my words entirely out of context and gave everything I said a sinister slant. I can't believe that I could be as naive as to trust that little bitch!"

"Don't blame yourself, Luisa. I was taken in as much as you were. Tanya is the daughter of a friend of mine, but I never would have allowed her to sit in if I'd known what she had in mind. I know her mother would never have asked me to allow Tanya to cover the story contest for her paper if Jean had any inkling that it would lead to this."

"Be that as it may, Miranda, the hospital board of trustees has decided to investigate my background in the light of these charges and have asked me to take a leave of absence while they do it."

"I can't believe it! How could they be such craven cowards as not to back you up one hundred per cent? Don't they realize what a terrific job you're doing?"

"I guess that all amounts to nothing when the muckrakers make wild accusations. In any case, Ernie and I have decided to take a vacation until the investigation is completed. After that, well…we'll see."

"I'm sure they won't find anything in your background to support these ludicrous charges, Luisa. You are coming back to Dos Hermanas, aren't you?"

"Of course we'll come back, Miranda, but whether or not I will return to work is still up in the air. I've been at DH Hospital for a very long time and I've been thinking about retiring. Perhaps this is a sign that I should. I am terribly hurt by this whole sorry episode. In a way, it's my own fault. I should never have entered that particular story in the contest."

"But it's just a story, isn't it? You made it up especially for the contest, just like the other contestants did. How can that be wrong?"

"If that were the case, Miranda, you'd be correct. But you see, it isn't. I've avoided answering people when they asked me if it was true, but the fact is, everything I wrote was the absolute truth."

Miranda was dumfounded. For a moment, she couldn't speak. Then her good sense returned. After all, Luisa's story was no stranger than her own. The only difference was that Miranda had always kept her spiritual beliefs and practices to herself. Of course, Joseph knew and supported her, but other than that, it was purely her own business.

"If I were you, Luisa, I would not admit that to anyone. Just let it be our secret, okay?

"Is there anything I can do to help you, Luisa? I feel responsible in a way. After all, the contest was my idea. If I hadn't decided to sponsor it, none of this would have happened."

"My dear Miranda, please don't blame yourself for the irresponsible actions of another. We can't stop living just because someone may cause a problem. Nothing worth achieving would ever happen if we did…I can't think of anything you can do right now, Miranda. I have a sense that I should not respond to these charges. I don't want people to think I take them seriously."

Miranda sighed, "Of course you're right, Luisa. I'll think it through. I may decide to write a letter to the editor of 'The Braggart.' If I do, I'll save you a copy."

"Okay. Thanks, Miranda. I'll call you when we get back from Hawaii."

As Miranda replaced the receiver in its cradle, she sighed wearily. Her shoulders sagged and her head seemed suddenly heavy and burdensome. She allowed it to fall forward so that her chin rested on her chest. She could feel hot tears gathering behind her eyelids, and when they started to roll down her cheeks, she did nothing to stop them.

"I thought I was doing a good thing for the people of Dos Hermanas," she thought. "Instead, the whole thing has turned sour. How could the child of such a gentle mother be so heartless and cruel?"

She shook her head slowly from side to side and then reached for a Kleenex to mop up her tears and blow her nose.

"I don't know; sometimes things get so complicated. What to do? It's too late to cancel the contest. How could I explain to the finalists, not to mention the judges and everybody else who worked so hard to create this event? I don't know…I just don't know."

"Well now, isn't that just too bad…Feeling sorry for yourself, are you?

The raspy old lady's voice startled Miranda. It seemed to emanate from nowhere and everywhere at the same time.

"Giving up already? At the first bump in the road? Tch, tch, I thought you were made of sterner stuff, Miranda. Thinking about quitting, are you? Well then, you might just as well roll over and die!"

Miranda looked all around her, but could see no one.

"Hecate, where are you? I can hear you, but I don't see you. Where are you? And why are you being so mean?"

At that, Miranda heard an insistent tap-tap-tapping on the window of the cafe. She turned toward the sound and could just make out a dim, hooded figure outside the door. She went to the door and unlocked it. Then she slipped outside into the darkness. A low cackling laugh led her to its source. Hecate waited for her just around the corner of the building.

"Grandmother," Miranda addressed her respectfully, "Why are you so unkind to me? I need help, not a scolding."

"I'll be the judge of that, Miranda!" replied Hecate tartly. "It seems to me you haven't really given this turn of events your full attention. If you had, you'd know what to do!"

"Yes, Ma'am," Miranda accepted the rebuke meekly. "Have you any suggestions, wise one?"

"Well, you might start by writing that letter to the editor."

"Yes, and then what?"

"How should I know? I'm just a mean old woman! You said so yourself."

"I'm sorry, Hecate, I meant no disrespect. It's just that I feel so frustrated. I've tried calling Tanya several times. She's not answering the phone and she doesn't respond to the messages I left. I also called her mother, but Jean is visiting out of town relatives. She won't be back until next week. What else can I do?"

"Sometimes, the best thing to do is to wait and let the story write its own ending."

"Huh? I mean, I beg your pardon?" queried Miranda. "I don't get it."

"You will know the way to go when you get there, Miranda. You'll see. Have courage and trust your instincts. They have not led you astray."

As suddenly as Hecate had materialized, she disappeared, leaving Miranda to puzzle out her meaning. She stood quietly for moment thinking, and then she shrugged and turned back into the cafe, locking the door behind her.

However, things suddenly didn't seem so terrible. Miranda went back into the kitchen, her step lively and purposeful once more. She selected a crusty, round loaf of sesame seeded sourdough bread and sliced off the top. Then she removed most of the soft center. Opening the large refrigerator, Miranda found a container of left over goulash. She popped it into the microwave and zapped it. When it was bubbling hot and fragrant with garlic and paprika, she spooned it into the bread bowl she had made and then replaced the top of the loaf and secured it with toothpicks. After wrapping it in heavy aluminum foil, she placed it on the counter next to her purse. She put on her heavy cardigan sweater and slung her purse over her shoulder. Then she took her package and locking the door behind her, went out into the parking area. She placed the warm food on the passenger seat of her Toyota and started the motor.

"Time to go home, Miranda," she said aloud, "with just a short stop along the way."

As she drove, she hummed a simple tune. When she reached "her" clearing, she climbed out of the pick-up and glanced around warily. There was no one there, but she left the motor running, just in case…She took the foil wrapped package and went to the edge of the forest. She removed the foil, crumpled it up and placed it in her pocket. Then, she removed the toothpicks and placed the stew filled loaf on a couple of large leaves she found there. When she was satisfied with her gift, she spoke softly but clearly.

"Blessed be my friend, my sister, my rescuer. Enjoy this food which I have prepared for you, with a hearty appetite."

Arlene Spector

Although Miranda could not see her forest friend, she sensed that the she-wolf was not far off. Miranda turned away and started out once more toward home and Joseph.

In the forest, a pair of golden eyes watched and a moist muzzle twitched at the delicious aroma emanating from the forest's edge. The old she-wolf padded quietly to the edge of the clearing and accepted Miranda's gift.

CHAPTER ELEVEN

There is an ancient Greek legend about a strange and evil creature named "Medusa." She had the face of a beautiful woman, but instead of a lovely head of hair to match, the gods gave her a writhing nest of poisonous serpents. She sat on a rock in the sea, and sang beautiful songs and cajoled innocent seafarers to look upon her face. If they succumbed, they were instantly turned to stone! It took a wise and courageous hero, Odysseus, to beat her at her own game. He held up his polished shield, and Medusa was forced to look at her own reflection.

The Storysmith

* * * * * * * * *

Miranda reread her letter one last time before placing it into its envelope:

Letters to the Editor
The Braggart Newspaper
Fort Bragg, California
Dear Editor:

As the proprietor of "Miranda's Cafe" and the sponsor of the first annual Dos Hermanas short story contest, I must object to the distorted treatment given to this event by your reporter Tanya McCullough.

Specifically, I refer to her story about one of the finalists, Luisa Marino and her short story entitled "The Witch and the Engineer." Your reporter has presented Ms. Marino's imaginative tale as though it were a true story rather than a work of fiction. Furthermore, the details of the story were twisted in such a way as to suggest wrongdoing on the part of Ms. Marino, who happens to be a highly respected professional nurse and administrator at our local hospital.

Had I been informed of your reporter's intention to create a scandal out of an innocent entertainment, I would not have agreed to allow her to cover any of the presentations by our finalists. This is yellow journalism at its worst! Please print a retraction as soon as possible.

> Very Truly Yours,
> Miranda of Miranda's Cafe

"Well," said Miranda, "Short of threatening to sue, that's as strong as I can make it. I hope it does the job."
"I wouldn't bet on it if I were you, Miranda," said Joseph. 'The Braggart' thrives on scandal and innuendo."
"You're absolutely right on that, Joseph, but I've got to take some action. I can't just stand by and watch a fine person like Luisa get in trouble just because she entered our short story contest."
"I agree wholeheartedly, Miranda, but my expectation is that they won't print your letter. What then?"
"Joseph, I honestly don't know. I'll have to play it by ear…Any suggestions?"

Joseph leaned back in his chair and placed the tips of his fingers together, his thumbs resting under his chin. He let out a big sigh and closed his eyes. Miranda knew that he was searching his mind for possible solutions to the dilemma. Finally, he looked up at her; his blue eyes wide open now.

"Have you spoken to Tanya's mother yet?"

"I've been trying to reach her, but she's been out of town and her answering machine is full up. I did get to leave one message asking her to call me when she gets back."

Joseph nodded, "Well, until she does, I guess there's not much we can do. I was thinking that we could contact the Dos Hermanas Hospital Board of Trustees, but that might do more harm than good by making it seem too important. I'm sure their investigation will find nothing to be concerned about."

"I hope you're right," agreed Miranda.

"You don't sound too sure, my dear. Is there something you haven't told me?" asked Joseph.

"You're much too perceptive, Joseph. I might have guessed that I wouldn't be able to keep a secret around you," she complained.

"Never mind the flattery, Miranda." he replied, "Are you going to tell me or not?"

Miranda burst out laughing. "If I said: 'Not', would you let me get away with it?"

"No," he answered, and put his arms around her. "I shan't let go until you tell me your guilty secret," upon which he began tickling her in the ribs. She broke into giggles and struggled to escape, but Joseph's grip was too strong. Finally, she gave in.

"Okay, okay, okay, I'll talk, but let me catch my breath."

Finally, she took a large breath of air and confessed.

"Luisa Marino told me, in strict confidence, that her story is absolutely true. I advised her to keep that secret, and assured her that I will, too. Obviously that extends to you."

Joseph nodded in agreement, "I'd say that was good advice, Miranda, and you can count on me to respect your confidence, seeing as how I wrested it from you under duress." Miranda smiled and gathered up her outgoing mail, including the letter to editor of 'The Braggart.'

"I'd say 'Wrestled' is closer to the truth, Joseph!" she retorted.

He smiled and nodded somewhat sheepishly. "Caught red-handed again!"

Miranda continued: "Now, could you to stop at the main post office to mail these letters for me? I'm sending a copy of my letter to Jean, with a note. I don't want her to think I blame her for Tanya's story.

"Good thought. I have a feeling this isn't the first time that Tanya has created trouble for someone."

* * * * * * * * *

On Thursday, Miranda waited anxiously for the current copy of "The Braggart" to arrive at the cafe.

"That's a first for you, Miranda," observed Ruthie. "Usually that dirty rag gets thrown in the trash unread."

"As it so richly deserves," added Miranda, "And I wouldn't be reading it today except that I want to see if they printed my letter to the editor."

Miranda shuffled quickly through the pile of mail, setting the first class envelopes to one side to be read later.

Finally, she found what she was looking for. She carried "The Braggart" over to the nearest table, sat down and without even glancing at the first page, she turned quickly to the "Letters to the Editor" section.

"Damn! Those lily-livered cowards didn't print my letter. What a bunch of low-lives!"

"Just what you'd expect from a scandal sheet like that one," added Ruthie. "What now?"

"I don't know," Miranda replied sadly. "It's so unfair for someone as decent as Luisa Marino to have to put up with this sort of thing...To think that the hospital board has chosen to dignify this crap by investigating her. I honestly don't understand it."

"Well then, perhaps you should write to them, instead," opined Ruthie.

"I would, except that Luisa asked me not to."

Ruthie nodded. "Shall I put this carrion in the trash bin, where it belongs?"

Miranda nodded, "Uh-huh," and headed for the kitchen.

Ruthie picked the offending publication off the table between her thumb and her forefinger and carried it like some disease bearing piece of filth to the wastebasket. Just as she was about to deposit it, something caught her eye. She glanced at the headline and stopped short.

"Miranda, come look at this, will you! That pack of vermin has really gone off the deep end this time. You won't believe it! Next thing, we'll be having alien babies growin' in the cabbage patch!"

Miranda turned and took the tabloid from Ruthie's hand. She perused page one quickly and read aloud:

"MORE WITCHCRAFT IN DOS HERMANAS?"

The headline in bold black letters seemed to scream at her. She read further: "Two Fort Bragg youths reported to local police of a strange occurrence last Sunday night at about nine p.m. They said that they had pulled off the road when they saw a pick-up truck stranded by the side of the road, with an elderly woman standing next to it. When they stopped to offer assistance, however, she turned on them. They reported that she screamed horrible curses and what sounded to them like an evil incantation. Then she disappeared and in her place was a large gray wolf, frothing at the mouth with 'an unholy light in its eyes,' according to one of the young men. It growled fiercely, they reported, and as they turned and ran toward their vehicle, it chased after them. When they had made it safely into their car and locked the doors, the animal leaped onto the hood and continued to threaten them through the windshield. As they drove off in a panic, their momentum caused her to slide off onto the road.

"'It was really scary,' said one of the youths. 'That creature from hell kept chasing our car until we floored it and got away.' They appeared to be badly shaken, although uninjured, when they reported their experience to local police, and asked not to be identified by name for fear that the witch, who resembled a local cafe owner, might seek revenge."

The by-line read, "Tanya McCullough, staff reporter."

"What a pack of lies!" said Miranda, shaking her head, "What's next? Maybe she'll demand that Luisa and I be burned at the stake!"

"That brat has certainly lost her marbles this time," said Ruthie. "As if anyone in their right mind would believe such nonsense."

Miranda was startled by Ruthie's reaction. Then she remembered that she hadn't told anyone but Joseph what had happened that night.

"Perhaps it's better just to leave it that way," she thought. "There's nothing to be gained from lending Tanya's twisted tale credence."

"Ruthie, my dear, if that were true, I'd have nothing to worry about," said Miranda. "Unfortunately, there are always people willing to believe the worst, no matter how absurd."

Miranda shook her head and made her way to the kitchen. Ruthie picked up "The Braggart" and crumpled it, before tossing into the trash bin with a snort of derision.

Ten minutes hadn't gone by before they heard the tinkle of the front door bell announcing the arrival of a patron. Miranda wiped her hands on a paper towel and went to greet the new arrival. It was Jean McCullough, Tanya's mother.

"Oh, Jean, I'm so glad to see you. I've been trying to get hold of you by phone."

"Yes, I got your message the minute I got back in town, but rather than call you, I thought it would be better to see you in person. I can't tell you how upset I am. I read Tanya's articles in "The Braggart". Oh, Miranda, I am so sorry! If I'd had any inkling that she would behave so badly, I'd never have asked you to allow her to report on the contest."

With that, Jean burst into tears and stood there so forlornly that it nearly broke Miranda's heart to see how distraught she was. Miranda went to her and put her arms around Jean.

"Jean, I don't blame you for your daughter's actions. It was obvious to me that you knew nothing of what she intended. I never for one moment thought that you did. Please, sit down while I get us some coffee. We can talk when you are a little calmer."

She led Jean to a table toward the back of the dining room and pulled out a chair for her. Jean had pulled out a handkerchief and was wiping her eyes and blowing her nose as she tried to calm down. Miranda went to get coffee. She returned quickly with a carafe and two cups. After she had set them down and poured coffee for both of them, Miranda sat down with Jean and took both of Jean's small hands in her own. They were ice cold. Miranda rubbed them gently and waited for Jean to talk. Jean took a deep breath and was finally able to speak coherently.

"I am so ashamed. You are kind, Miranda, to say that I am not to blame, but I'm afraid that's not so. I raised Tanya and I'm afraid I didn't do a very good job of it."

Miranda remained silent, waiting for Jean to unburden herself.

"Once, I told you about my childhood in the internment camp. I guess I never did get over those nightmare years. When I found out I was pregnant with Tanya, I was determined that my child would have the wonderful childhood I was denied. She would not suffer, as we did, from hunger or cold or the denigration of being locked up, not because of anything we had done, but only because we were of Japanese origin. I didn't want my child to have to go through that, and when she was born with red hair and light eyes, I was happy that no one would mistake her for an Asian child. That's how deeply my self-hatred went!

"I saw to it that Tanya had everything, pretty dresses, piano lessons and dance lessons, and toys enough to start a toy store. There was nothing she asked for that she didn't get. When she went to high school, we entertained her friends at our house whenever she wanted it. We paid her way through college, and we were pleased when she finally settled on a career in Journalism. We praised her every small accomplishment, hoping to encourage her to do well, without ever insisting that she try harder. So you see, Miranda, with all our good intentions, her father and I created a child who thinks only of herself and what she wants. She never had to suffer the consequences of her own actions.

"We have only ourselves to blame, Miranda. We thought that if we were kind and loving and generous to our daughter, she would grow up to be a kind and generous and loving young woman. Instead, she learned to be a person who takes and takes and takes, and gives nothing but heartache in return. I have been trying to reach her, but she must be screening her calls; I went to her apartment, but she wasn't there. When I called the offices of "The Braggart," they said she wasn't there, either.

"Jean, I don't know what to tell you. I wrote a letter of protest to the editor, but they didn't bother to print it. I'm not concerned about their silly accusations against me, but I am concerned about Luisa Marino. The Board of Trustees of the hospital are investigating the allegations of witchcraft against Luisa and have asked her to take administrative leave until they are through."

There was dead silence while Jean digested this new piece of information.

"How ridiculous to think that Luisa would ever do harm. Anyone who knows her knows that!" Jean shook her head again.

"I agree," said Miranda, "but the fact remains that the investigation has begun; Luisa has gone on leave and she is seriously considering early retirement. That's how hurt she is by all this."

"That's terrible! What can I do? Should I write to the Board or appear before them? I'll do anything you suggest, Miranda."

Miranda took a sip of her coffee. "It's not that simple, Jean. But perhaps there is something you can do."

"Anything, Miranda, just tell me what it is."

"Okay, but first hear me out before you agree. I do appreciate your good intentions, but it may not be easy for you."

"I'm listening," replied Jean.

"Okay, then, but drink your coffee before it gets cold."

Miranda poured them each another cup from the carafe. "Jean, I appreciate your desire to set things right, but I don't think it's up to you to atone for your daughter's sins. In my opinion, it's long past time for Tanya to deal with the consequences of her own actions. For starters, she needs to learn something about ethics, whether as a journalist or simply a decent human being. However, while I don't think working for 'The Braggart' is likely to teach her anything good in that direction, I think it would be a big mistake to get her fired."

"You're probably right, Miranda," agreed Jean. "It would only make her angrier and more rebellious, if I know my daughter…But what else can we do?"

Miranda's Muse

"Jean, do you think you could persuade Tanya to come next Sunday to the awards presentation reception here at the cafe?"

Jean paused and thought about it for a moment. Then, she replied with fresh determination in her voice: "I will get her here, if I have to drug her to do it! You can rely on that, Miranda. I've had about enough of her thoughtless and malicious behavior!"

Miranda smiled. "It would probably be better if she were fully conscious, Jean, but I get your drift."

"What have you got in mind, Miranda, if you don't mind my asking?"

"No, of course I don't mind your asking, Jean, but I'm not sure myself yet, as to what to do. I've got an inkling, but I haven't thought it all the way through. In any case, I think it'll be better if you know nothing in advance. Can you handle that?"

"Miranda, I trust you to do what's right."

"Thank you Jean; that means a lot to me."

After Jean left the cafe, Miranda went back into the kitchen. Ruthie saw the expression on her face and recognized that Miranda was lost in her own thoughts.

"Better not to interrupt Miranda when she's thinking," she told herself. "She's figuring out what to do if I know Miranda at all."

Finally, Miranda broke the silence.

"Who's coming in today, Ruthie?"

Ruthie thought for a moment and then went to the chart on the bulletin board near the door to check.

"Ah, I thought so. Irene is due in at eleven-thirty, Miranda. Then Danny will be here by three."

"Well, I'll wait until Irene arrives. Then I have some business to attend to, Ruthie. I may not be back in time for dinner preparations. Can the three of you manage without me?"

"Of course we can, Miranda," replied Ruthie. "Don't worry about a thing."

*   *   *   *   *   *   *   *   *

Joseph was surprised when he arrived home at six o'clock to find Miranda waiting for him.

She had set the table and Joseph could smell the delicious aroma of a roasting chicken.

After greeting her with a hug and a kiss, he asked: "To what do I owe the honor of your charming presence at such an early hour, gracious lady? And with dinner prepared by your own dainty little hands?"

Miranda laughed. "Fooled you, didn't I? Well, to be honest, I just got home a half hour ago myself and I brought dinner with me from that new gourmet market in Fort Bragg, 'Elegant Eats.' I put the chicken in the oven to keep warm, and everything else is waiting to be zapped in the microwave, except for dessert, which is a surprise."

"Oh, did you tire of your own cooking, my dear?"

"Never that, Joseph, although I probably wouldn't admit that even if it were true. The fact is, I've been busily chasing from Dos Hermanas to Fort Bragg and decided to come straight home from there, rather than stopping back at the cafe…Now go wash up and I'll get supper on the table."

After the supper dishes had been cleared, Miranda and Joseph sat comfortably over coffee and her surprise dessert, which turned out to be real custard filled chocolate glazed éclairs from the French Patisserie in Fort Bragg.

"I don't imagine that your only reason for driving all the way to Fort Bragg was to bring me this éclair, Miranda…I do appreciate it, my dear, but that's a long way to go for a pastry, wouldn't you say?"

"Well, yes, it is a long way, Joseph and you're right, it wasn't my only reason for going there. My other reason was to get some good professional advice from Barbara Neuberger, publisher and editor of "The Sentinel."

"She's a very ethical journalist, and though I don't always see eye-to-eye with her editorials, she's a very insightful person, especially when it comes to the newspaper she runs. I told her about the Tanya McCullough situation and the problem her story created for Luisa Marino. She was able to clarify the issues involved in dealing with tabloids like "The Braggart."

"Did she have any recommendations?" asked Joseph.

"In a way. I'm dealing with two conflicting motives. On the one hand, I'd love to give Tanya the same kind of treatment she gave Luisa, but I don't want to do anything to hurt Jean."

Joseph shook his head doubtfully from side to side.

"I wouldn't want to walk that tightrope, my dear. What happens if your foot slips?"

"I guess I'd fall off, and that's why I'm asking for advice."

"Are you asking me, Miranda? Because, if you are, I don't know what to tell you."

"Well, yes, I am asking you to think about it and when you're ready, tell me your opinion."

"When will you need to know, Miranda?" asked Joseph.

"As soon as possible, but no later than the day before the prizes are awarded."

Joseph nodded, and then, almost as an afterthought, he asked, "Have you consulted the goddess, my dear?"

"That's my next step, Joseph, and part of the reason I came home early."

*   *   *   *   *   *   *   *   *

Later on, after Miranda had bathed and changed into a soft blue caftan and slippers, she parted the curtains in her bedroom and gazed out at the garden. The wind had come up and dark clouds were scudding swiftly across the face of the moon. Dark shadows alternated with brief flashes of moonlight. The foliage on the tall trees nearby was tossed roughly from side to side by gusts of a chilly wind. It seemed to Miranda that the trees were shaking their heads vehemently from side to side, warning her to stay within the shelter of her home. She nodded a silent acknowledgment and turned away from the window.

Seating herself on the edge of her bed, she waited, her mind open to whatever would come to her. For a while, bits and pieces of the day tumbled helter-skelter across the wide stage of her imagination. Then, without her willing it, Tanya's face exploded onto her mind-screen. There was a malicious glint in those strange green eyes and Tanya's mouth was distorted into a downward curve of disdain. Miranda drew her breath in sharply.

Then, without volition, anger welled up in Miranda's throat like a flood of hot acid. She sprang to her feet and clenched her teeth and her fists. Her body went rigid and everything she could see turned a searing scarlet for a brief moment.

"Oh my God!" she exclaimed, not knowing what she was saying. It was not a plea for help. That would come later. Nevertheless, the quiet voice within her spoke.

"I am here, Miranda and I will not abandon you."

At the sound of the gentle reminder Miranda released her breath and unclenched her fists. Her body relaxed and she sat down heavily on the side of her bed. She focused on her breathing, slowing it down and monitoring each breath until reflex took over.

"What just happened?" she asked. "I've never felt anything like that before. Please, tell me what that was," she begged.

"That dear child was rage, pure, unmitigated, poisonous rage. That was anger taken to its furthest extremity. You are right to be frightened. That sort of rage is beyond your ken. It will stop at nothing once it starts to burn."

"Why did it happen to me? I don't understand"

"I know that, Miranda. You have never harbored that kind of animosity toward anyone. That is why I caused you to experience it…Those horrendous emotions belong to Tanya. Only when she confronts herself and re writes the negative life script she has created, will she find redemption."

The voice of the goddess started to fade, as she said her last word on the subject:

"Hold up a mirror, Miranda, and let her see who she is," and suddenly she was gone.

CHAPTER TWELVE

"*Thus shall you say to the house of Jacob and declare to the children of Israel: 'You have seen what I did to the Egyptians, and how I bore you on eagles' wings and brought you to Me. Now then, if you will obey Me faithfully and keep My covenant, you shall be my treasured possession among all peoples. Indeed, all the earth is Mine, but you shall be a kingdom of priests and a holy nation.'" Exodus 19: 3-6*

Would God have selected the Jews to be "The Chosen People" if He'd known what trouble it would cause them?

The Storysmith

'*If there were no Jews, the anti-Semites would invent them.*"

Jean Paul Sartre
"Anti-Semite and Jew"

* * * * * * * * *

It had been several years since Miranda had dreamt this dream. It never came to disturb her slumber when things were going well, only when there was trouble. It always began the same way: Suddenly, all the rules were suspended! Nothing did what was expected. Miranda dropped a book, and it flew up to the ceiling. She looked out of a window and saw that the sun had not risen as it always had in the past. The whole world was as black as midnight. When she walked out of the front door, there was nothing but hard earth and black water all the way to the horizon. All the neighboring houses were gone and Miranda was alone on a flat plane that was barren of life.

"Please," she called out, "where are you? Somebody? Please answer me!"

There was no answer, just the echo of her own words mocking her. She strode out and made for the horizon, but the faster she walked, the more quickly the horizon receded.

"Where is everyone?" she wondered. "Where is Joseph? I need him. I'm scared!"

"No, tell the truth, Miranda…you're terrified!"

Her inner voice was relentless, as always, insisting on the truth. But what was the truth? Miranda didn't know anymore.

"In a time of chaos," an ancient voice told her, "the old truths are gone and the new ones have not yet been discovered. Everything happens for the first time, but may not follow the same rule again," and she heard a familiar raucous cackle.

"Hecate! Oh, Hecate" she cried, "Wonderful Hecate, I'm so glad to hear your voice!"

Hecate ignored her and continued preaching in her raspy old woman voice,

"Commit a crime and go to jail…Not any more, no more…" she crowed. "Kill or steal or burn down a city, and the world will love you for it!" She howled and broke into mirthless laughter. "The victim is at fault! If there were no victims, there would be no perpetrators!"

The crone did a strange little dance, shuffling and bobbing and bringing her staff down so hard, it left marks in the naked earth.

"Children hate parents…the kinder the mother, the more hateful the children! Abuse your babies and they will love you the better for it! Ugliness is beautiful, and misery divine! Kindness and gentleness are outlawed!" and she doubled over in a paroxysm of shrill hysteria.

"But don't depend on it," she continued as she straightened up once more, "Everything could change at any moment!" And, as suddenly as she had come, Hecate disappeared.

Miranda was frozen in place and time. She wanted to scream, but no sound issued from her lips. Her heart pounded wildly within her chest. She could hear the blood pulsing through her temples.

"Help me!" she prayed silently. "Help me, my Goddess!" she prayed again. "Help me, Gaia, Shekinah, Ashtoroth," she implored, calling upon all the names of the Deity she could remember.

Suddenly everything was still. A pool of clear water sparkled in front of Miranda. Standing in the pool was an antelope. Her soft dark eyes gazed at Miranda solemnly. The large furred ears perked up and turned toward her. She gazed at Miranda as though inspecting this strange trembling creature before her. Miranda moved slowly toward the antelope, and when she had come close, began to stroke the dark stripe down the antelope's back. The coarse hair felt good to Miranda's damp palms. She ran her hand up the graceful neck to the sharp points on the end of the twisted horns. The antelope stood absolutely still under Miranda's tender touch, and then turned her head to look deep into Miranda's eyes. Although the lovely creature made no audible sound, Miranda could hear a familiar gentle voice speaking to her.

"Rest easy, Miranda," she whispered, "You will live! You will survive and you will carve order out of chaos. Climb on my back and I will run like the wind until we are high above the earth. Then you will know chaos for what it truly is, a pattern that you cannot see because you are trapped within it. As we fly with the clouds and cross over the face of the moon, you will finally comprehend the whole magnificent pattern of existence, the delicately wrought design that encompasses all creation.

"Ah, Miranda, my child, don't you see? You already know everything!" and she was gone.

Miranda felt the sacred words take hold of her body and mind. Her fear melted into a reverent calm. All awareness faded away and Miranda moved deeper and deeper into restful slumber, beyond the reach of dreams.

* * * * * * * * *

At first, Miranda thought it was the alarm clock that woke her up so early. Then she remembered that she didn't have an alarm clock. She preferred waking up to soft music, rather than the raucous scream of an old fashioned alarm clock. She sat up and reached over to pick up the phone on her nightstand.

"Hello? Who's there?"

"Sorry to wake you so early, Miranda. This is Charley Perez...you know...Chief of Police?"

"Oh, of course, Charley. What's up? Is anything wrong?"

"Well, yes there is, Miranda. I wanted to get hold of you before you left for the cafe. It seems that somebody thought it would be fun to spray paint graffiti on the front of the cafe. So it's looking kind of messy now. I didn't want you to get a shock when you came in."

Miranda breathed a deep sigh before answering.

"Thanks, Charley, I appreciate that. Was there any other damage?"

"Well, yeah. They also threw a rock through your front door. I have one of my men guarding the place until you get here."

"I'll get dressed and be right there, Chief."

"Prepare yourself, Miranda. They wrote some pretty nasty stuff."

"Like what, Charley?" she asked.

"I'd rather not say, Miranda. It's about as vicious as I've ever seen...hateful language I'd just as soon not repeat."

"That bad, huh? Well, thanks for the warning. I'll expect the worst. Anybody see who did it?"

"Yeah, an early jogger spotted a beat up old car pulling out of the cafe parking lot and managed to remember the license number, so we shouldn't have any trouble rounding 'em up."

"Thanks again, Charley," said Miranda and hung up the phone.

Miranda rose and slid her feet into her slippers. Joseph was leaning back against his pillow watching her as she put on her robe.

"What's wrong, Miranda?"

"That was Charley Perez."

"The police chief? What happened?"

"Someone graffitied the cafe and threw a rock through the front door, Joseph. I'm going to grab a cup of coffee and get right down there."

Joseph got up and reached for his robe.

"I'm going with you, Miranda. I have a feeling you might need help when you get there."

"I'd appreciate it, Joseph. Charley said they wrote some pretty vicious things. He didn't care to repeat them so they must be terrible."

"Any idea who did it, Miranda?"

"They got the license number of the car, but they haven't arrested them yet. I'd be willing to bet it's the same bastards who accosted me that night when the wolf came to my rescue."

"You mean the same two that told that ridiculous story about a witch who changed herself into a wolf?" Joseph grinned mischievously. "Those two?"

Miranda smiled back.

"Yup. The very same."

"Well, they're really in for it now; breaking and entering, malicious mischief and who knows what other charges? For sure now, no one will believe that story they told about you."

* * * * * * * * *

As Miranda and Joseph pulled up in front of the cafe, Miranda's jaw dropped. It was far worse than she had imagined. Smeared across the front of the cafe in bright red and black spray paint were the words:

"BURN IN HELL WITCH...HITLER WAS RIGHT...DIE JEW BITCH"

There were swastikas and obscenities scribbled at random in the same crude lettering. Miranda got out of Joseph's car and stood looking at the desecration of this special place she loved so much. She felt an icy chill between her shoulder blades.

"This is my 'Crystallnacht,'" she thought, remembering the vicious attack by the Nazis on Jewish shops just before World War II broke out. She covered her eyes with her hands. Hot tears began to roll down her face.

"I don't understand. It makes no sense…What have I done to deserve such hatred from people I don't even know?" she asked.

Her inner voice replied, "It is not what you have done, Miranda; It is who you are and what you stand for."

Terror, like an ice-cold dagger, thrust into her gut. She crossed her arms and hugged herself for comfort. After Joseph had pulled his car into the cafe parking lot, he returned to the street side of the cafe. When he saw Miranda standing there, with her head bowed, her body shaking with fear, he ran to her and took her in his arms.

"Miranda, darling, don't be afraid! I'm here for you. I won't let anybody harm you. It'll be okay. We'll clean this mess up right away. You'll see. It'll be like it never happened!"

Miranda accepted the warmth of Joseph's embrace gratefully. She couldn't speak, but she shook her head. Finally, the words came out of her.

"Some things cannot be forgotten, Joseph. This is one of them."

Miranda hugged Joseph with all her strength and then stepped back and looked at his sweet familiar countenance, his forehead wrinkled with concern for her.

"Thank you for being here Joseph," she said simply, "when I need you so desperately."

She smiled and looked deeply into the blue eyes she loved so much. What she saw there gave her the courage she needed to tackle the task ahead.

Ruthie arrived just then and parked her car in her usual space. She came around the front of the cafe and surveyed the damage.

"God, almighty, what has happened here?" exclaimed Ruthie. "Who could have done such a turrrible dirrrty thing?"

Her Irish brogue always intensified when Ruthie was upset.

Joseph turned toward her and answered. "I don't know, but I understand they got a license plate number, Ruthie. By the way, 'Good Morning, if it is a good morning, which I doubt.'"

The line from "Winnie the Pooh" sounded oddly incongruous in this setting, Joseph thought, and wondered why he'd chosen just those words. He shrugged. They seemed to lessen the impact of the morning's events. "Thank God," he thought, "for the healing balm of gentle humor."

At this point, Miranda had gone over to the officer who had been stationed there to guard the cafe. Joseph came over and joined her there.

"Thank you for being here, officer" she said. "Come inside for a cup of coffee and a sweet roll before you go back to work."

"No, thank you Ma'am" he replied. "I need to report back to the Chief now." He turned, climbed onto his motorcycle and took off in the direction of the station house.

Miranda and Joseph watched him leave in silence. Miranda let out a deep sigh, and then shrugged her shoulders.

"I don't understand this" she commented. "I just don't get it. People who've had their houses broken into talk about feeling violated. Now I know how they feel."

"I know, Miranda. It seems like such a stupid and pointless thing to do. What a waste of time and energy. You'd think the young would have better things to do than create this ugliness."

"Well, be that as it may, Joseph, what now?"

"Now, my dear Miranda, we get to work. Do we still have some paint left over from the last time we had the cafe painted?"

"I think so. It's in back, in the garden shed. There should be a couple of brushes there too."

"Okay, I'll check it out and bring whatever we have to the front of the cafe. Why don't you get started in the kitchen? Your early birds will be in soon and they'll have a lot to talk about."

Miranda turned and headed toward the back door. It felt so good to have Joseph taking over this way. As she reached for the doorknob, Danny pulled up, followed in her car by Irene. They got out and came toward Miranda.

"There was a news flash on the local radio station that someone had vandalized the cafe, so Mom and I came right down. Melanie will be here right after her first class."

"Thank you, Irene and Danny. Right now, we can use all the help we can get."

"Where do we begin, Miranda?" asked Irene.

"Come into the kitchen with Ruthie and me, Irene, while Danny helps Joseph."

Danny turned and headed toward where Joseph had already begun lining up the painting supplies.

"Oh, Danny, I'm glad you're here. Come with me over to Nussbaum's hardware store. I want to pick up some rollers and roller pans and a few plastic sheets to protect the bushes and the walkway."

"Right-o, Professor. I'll sweep up the broken glass and measure the door so we can replace the broken window pane."

* * * * * * * * *

An hour later, Joseph and Danny had everything they would need to repair the front of the cafe. By this time, the morning rush had begun and Miranda, Ruthie and Irene were busy cooking and serving breakfast.

The regulars were outraged by what had happened. They had lots of questions to ask of Miranda. She answered them as best she could, while keeping up the pace so that everyone was fed in a timely manner.

"Miranda," began old Mr. Taylor, "it looks to me like you could use some help to put the cafe back in good shape."

Miranda smiled at the old man.

"Right you are as usual, Mr. Taylor. I'm getting concerned because Joseph has to be at work at the university by noon, and I think Danny has classes this afternoon as well. I wouldn't want him to miss them."

Mr. Taylor stood up and addressed the other diners:

"Good morning ladies and gentlemen. I see a lot of familiar faces here this morning. I have a friendly invitation to deliver to all of you who are physically able:

Miranda is always here for us, whenever we need a good meal and some pleasant company. More than once, she's served up a free meal or made a mistake on the tab in favor of some poor fella or gal who didn't have a lot of money. Well, she's having a bit of trouble this morning, due to the rotten way some young folks behaved.

"Now, I am in my nineties, but I'm as fit an old codger as you're likely to find. I may have slowed down somewhat because of the 'arthuritis' in my knees and hands, but I can still hold a paintbrush. So, if you'll lend me an apron Miranda, I'm going out to help the Professor. Anybody else care to join me?"

There was a brief moment of silence and then, three men got up and called out, "I will."..."Me too!"..."Yeah, me too!"

Two sturdy looking women wearing fashionable slacks and jackets stood up and headed for the door.

"Sis and I are going home to change into our grungies and then we'll be back to help," said one of them. The other one nodded her agreement as they headed out the door and up the street.

As soon as she could, Miranda went out to the front of the cafe. Joseph, Danny, Mr. Taylor and the two women, now clad in faded blue jeans and oversized T-shirts, were busily painting over the graffiti with the same soft gray paint that covered the rest of the building.

"Where are the other volunteers?" she asked.

Joseph answered: "I sent them to pick up some smaller brushes to do the window frames."

Miranda turned away and started to head back into the cafe. As she did, a battered gray van pulled up in front of the cafe. Painted on the side was the legend, "Tony's

Quality Painting Service" and a phone number. The driver tooted the familiar rhythm of "dum-dum de dum dum, - dum dum," and jumped out of the driver's seat.

"Hi Miranda. Greetings Professor. I heard you got a bit of trouble here. Some jerks graffitied the cafe, eh? No problem, I'll paint it over…no charge for labor."

"That's really lovely of you, Tony. People have been just great; we have half a dozen volunteers, but we sure could use a team leader with your expertise. Joseph and Danny need to get back to the university pretty soon, so you've arrived in the nick of time."

"Okay, you just leave the rest to me and we'll be done in no time."

Joseph and Danny thanked Tony, put down their rollers and headed for the cafe to clean themselves up. Miranda returned to the kitchen.

"Ruthie, would you please make a tray of sandwiches for our painting crew? It's getting on toward lunch and they must be hungry by now."

"What kind should I make, Miranda?"

"How about ham and cheese on rye and tuna fish on whole wheat, so folks can have a choice. Also, bring out some cans of soda and paper cups."

"Consider it done, Miranda," replied Ruthie.

Tony was true to his word. With his expert help and direction, the cafe looked fresh and bright again by half past twelve. Ruthie brought out the sandwich tray and sodas and set them down on a table she'd brought outside. The volunteers crowded around and helped themselves. Then, they found places on the benches in front of the cafe and chatted over their lunch.

"There's nothing like a solid morning's work to give me an appetite," declared Mr. Taylor. The others agreed vociferously. When they were almost done, Miranda came out of the cafe and thanked each one personally.

"You have no idea," she began, "how much your neighborly spirit means to me. When I saw the way the cafe looked this morning, I was heartsick that someone could be capable of such hateful behavior. Your offers of help reminded me of the kinder side of human nature. I can't thank you enough."

Later on, Chief Charley Perez called Miranda to tell her that the perpetrators of the crime had been rounded up and were cooling their heels in the Fort Bragg police station pending charges of vandalism, malicious mischief, breaking and entering, and committing a hate crime.

"That's a serious federal crime, you know," he informed her.

"Thanks for keeping us informed, Charley," said Miranda. "Let me know if you need me as a witness, although I didn't actually see them do it."

"Not to worry, Miranda. Their car was filled with evidence—black and red spray paint cans, hate literature from that neo-Nazi group that's causing problems down South County, that sort of stuff. This isn't their first offense, either."

"After seeing the nature of the graffiti, I guess that's no big surprise, Charley."

"No, unfortunately it's not. Well, they've stepped over the line this time and I intend to see that they pay the price!"

"I hope so, Chief," said Miranda.

* * * * * * * * *

By the time that Sunday rolled around, everything seemed peaceful once again. Irene and Ruthie had outdone themselves, having baked enough pies to stock a pie shoppe. There were Granny Smith apple pies, tart and sweet and juicy with cinnamon and a dash of allspice. Irene had made Miranda's favorite rhubarb pie and Joseph's special lemon meringue. "I'd travel to the ends of the earth for one of Irene's Lemon 'Ma-ring-goo' pies," he declared while rolling his eyes toward heaven."

Miranda had decided to serve today's refreshments buffet style. Danny had set up one long table near the kitchen. It was covered in the cafe's signature blue and white checked tablecloth, with a large flower arrangement in the center of the table. The pies were arranged alternately so that folks wouldn't bunch up at one pie station. Plates and silverware were neatly arranged at both ends of the table, but the coffee cups were distributed among the small cafe tables. Miranda had decided to use colorful paper napkins rather than cloth today and Melanie had arranged them attractively, like fans, in the center of each of the individual tables.

"That looks so pretty, Mel, that I don't think we need centerpieces," remarked Miranda. Then she looked at her watch.

"Well, people should start arriving any moment now, so let's fill the carafes and place one on each small table, along with sugar and cream."

Melanie nodded. "Should I also bring a carafe of tea for each table, Miranda?"

"No, most of them prefer coffee and the few who prefer tea will ask for it."

Just as the clock struck three, the front door opened and the first guest made her appearance. It was Lucille Lorman. She and Miranda greeted each other with a hug and chatted for a few moments before the other guests started arriving.

"Welcome!" said Miranda. "Please help yourselves to pie and coffee." "Melanie, please bring out a gallon of vanilla ice cream to go on the fruit pies. Why don't you station yourself at the buffet table and scoop it out for our guests?"

The cheerful chatter of the assembled company soon filled the cafe. After everyone had served him or herself and were comfortably seated around the tables, Miranda started toward the microphone to begin the festivities.

*   *   *   *   *   *   *   *   *

Jean glanced at her watch for the fifth time in the last half hour. It was Sunday afternoon and Tanya had grudgingly agreed to meet her mother for coffee. Jean turned on her car radio and closed her eyes for a moment to rest them.

"How am I going to approach this rebellious child of mine? What can I say that will persuade her to do as I ask and attend the award ceremony at Miranda's Cafe?"

She shook her head and breathed a large sigh. As she thought about Tanya, she remembered the time when Tanya was about four years old. She had been a tiny sprite of a child, with red curls and green eyes that flashed when she was angry or excited about something, and she was almost always angry or excited. No doubt about it, she had definite opinions about everything and insisted upon having her own way. It took all Jean's ingenuity to convince her to accept a compromise for what was clearly impossible, dangerous or unhealthy.

"Tanya, you may not build a fire in the living room! We do not have a fire place."

Jean remembered ruefully how they had finally settled on building a fire in the barbecue pit in the backyard. She just didn't have the strength, after a full day's work to hold out against Tanya's tantrums. Her husband, Jim was no help either! When he came home from his job as an automobile salesman, all he wanted was a couple of martinis before dinner, and one or two brandies after. Talk about dysfunctional families…The McCullough's were a prime example, thought Jean ruefully; a father who's a drunk, and a weak mother full of self-hatred. It was no wonder that Tanya seemed to despise them so much of the time. If her mother and father had so little self-respect, how could Tanya respect them? The more generous they were, showering her with the latest toys advertised on television, the brattier she became. Jean's attempts to establish some kind of order met with dismal failure. She had no support from her husband and eventually, she gave up and gave in.

Tanya often had nightmares, Jean remembered. The child would wake up screaming, but unable to tell her concerned parents what she had dreamt that frightened her so. Her eyes would roll back like a panicked animal's and she would cover her mouth with her hands as she thrashed in Jean's arms. Eventually, Jean would be able to calm her to the point where she would relax and fall asleep on Jean's shoulder. Tanya never remembered that she had dreamt when she awoke in the morning.

"It was no wonder that Tanya had night terrors," thought Jean, "If a three year old could control us, how could she ever depend upon us to keep her safe?"

Just then, Tanya's car pulled into the slot ahead of Jean. Jean opened her car door and waited until Tanya got out of her car and saw her. Tanya walked toward her mother's car.

"What's up, Ma?" asked Tanya.

"I have something I'd like to discuss with you, Tanya." replied Jean.

Tanya rolled her eyes and breathed an impatient sigh.

"Oh, not another of your lectures!" she whined. "Must it be today?"

"Yes, Tanya, it has to be right now. In fact, it is long overdue!"

Tanya looked at her mother's face. There was a strength and determination there that Tanya couldn't remember ever seeing before. She breathed a big sigh and opened the car door and got into the passenger side. As Jean started the motor, Tanya adjusted her seat back so that she was lying as far back as possible. She closed her eyes and pretended to sleep. Jean glanced at her daughter's face and headed for Dos Hermanas.

When she reached Miranda's Cafe, Jean parked right in front, as close to the entrance as possible. At that moment, Tanya opened her eyes and realized where they were.

"What the hell! Mother, what do you think you're doing? There's no way I'm going in there!"

"I don't blame you for feeling uncomfortable about facing Miranda, after the rotten stunt you pulled on Luisa Marino! Well, my dear daughter, it's time you faced the consequences of your own lousy behavior. You are damn well going to face the music, if I have to knock you out and drag you!"

Tanya was astonished. She'd never seen her mother like this before. She reached for the door handle to get out and leave, but she couldn't get the door to open. Jean had activated the safety locks and none of the doors would open. Tanya saw Jean heading around the front of the car, keys in hand. When she got to the passenger side, Jean quickly unlocked and opened the door next to Tanya, grabbed her firmly by her wrist and pulled her out of the car. Tanya was astonished by her mother's strength. Her grip felt like a steel band encircling Tanya's wrist. Tanya realized that this time, she wasn't going to get her way. Sullenly she submitted to entering the cafe with Jean.

* * * * * * * * *

Just as Miranda was adjusting the height of the microphone, the front door of the cafe opened. It was Jean McCullough and true to her word, she had her daughter Tanya by the wrist. She reminded Miranda of a small, but determined tugboat towing a dark and forbidding pirate ship into the harbor. Jean had a firm grip on Tanya's wrist and it was clear from the girl's sullen demeanor that she did not want to be there. They took a seat at a table toward the back of the room. Miranda acknowledged their presence with a nod in Jean's direction, and turned to speak to Melanie at her station behind the buffet table.

"Mel, please ask the late arrivals what kind of pie they would like and serve them at their table. I'm going to begin the proceedings."

She seated herself on the storyteller's stool. The audience quieted down almost immediately, and listened eagerly to what Miranda was about to say.

"Greetings, one and all! The day we have all been awaiting has finally arrived. Today we will find out which of our finalists will win the coveted first place award, as well as the very honorable mention prizes. Each of our storytellers has done an outstanding job, not only by writing an original short story, but also in presenting it for our enjoyment. Before we get to the actual awarding of prizes, I'd like to introduce you to some of the people whose hard work and integrity have been so important to the success of this contest."

"First of all, it's my privilege to introduce our panel of judges. We chose them very carefully; each of them is a person of impeccable character and sound judgment. As I call your name, would you each please rise and accept the gratitude of all of us here for the fine job you did in selecting our finalists and for later overseeing the tabulation of the votes as indicated on the evaluation sheets we have passed out at each performance.

"In alphabetical order, let me first present Father Dimitri of Saint Sophia's Russian Orthodox Church."

A sturdily built man of average height, with a full growth of curly black beard and compelling dark eyes arose and accepted the applause of the crowd.

"Dr. Harold Johnson, our own Dean of Students at the University, will you please arise?"

A tall, slender man with sparse light brown hair and thick glasses stood up and took a bow.

"Rabbi Donald Moseson, of the Fort Bragg Jewish Center, please stand up and accept our thanks."

The Rabbi stood in his place. He looked young for such an important position, not more than thirty years old. A traditional 'yarmulke' sat on the back of his head and as he took a bow, it threatened to fall off his springy blond curls. He lifted a practiced hand to catch it and pressed it back into its proper place on his head.

"Professor Irene Schoenberg, please come out of the kitchen."

Irene bustled out of the kitchen, wiping her hands on a corner of her apron.

"Now, it was not our intention, when we were setting up the rules of this contest, to have a member of my crew here at the cafe be on the judges panel. However, Dr. Schoenberg was not at that time working here. After consulting with the other judges, it was decided that, since she does not have anyone participating in the competition, it would be permissible for her to be a judge for the purpose of breaking any tie votes. As a teacher of English and Creative Writing, her expertise was valuable to our panel."

The other judges all nodded their agreement enthusiastically as everyone clapped.

"And last alphabetically, but certainly not least, let me present Reverend Robert Wilson of the First Baptist Church, right here in Dos Hermanas."

Reverend Wilson, a studious looking, light complexioned black man arose and smiled at the group, before bowing and retaking his seat.

"Now, before we announce the results, there is someone well known to our community who would like to announce a special award. It's my pleasure to present Dr. Barbara Neuberger, owner and publisher of the "Fort Bragg Sentinel."

A large dignified looking woman with carefully coifed white hair arose from her seat and came up to the microphone. Barbara Neuberger wore an expensive looking navy suit over a white georgette tailored shirt with pearl buttons. Pearl stud earrings, navy stockings and sensible shoes completed her outfit.

"Good afternoon, ladies and gentlemen. First, I'd like to express my thanks to Miranda for allowing me the privilege of addressing you and presenting a special award to a deserving person.

"Miranda is a person for whom I have the utmost respect and affection, even though we rarely see eye to eye politically. If you are subscribers to my paper, you have probably figured that out for yourself; but just in case we have any here who do not read 'The Sentinel', allow me to inform you that Miranda falls into the political and philosophical position of 'moderate liberal,' while I must admit to being a 'moderate conservative.'

"However much we may disagree in some arenas, there are some places we stand shoulder to shoulder in agreement. I'd like to tell you of one of these before presenting this award.

"Miranda and I feel very strongly that we need to encourage and support our talented young people who have shown special ability in the arts. The ability to write prose, poetry, fiction and non-fiction should be treated with great respect as the way we transmit the best of our culture to current and future generations. But it is not enough, in my opinion, to encourage the use of these gifts without teaching that they are to be used and not abused. High moral and ethical standards should be taught and insisted upon in the realm of writing for the public, whether we are speaking of fiction or non-fiction.

"Unfortunately, not every publication seems to agree with my and Miranda's views in this matter. Fiction and non-fiction are often mixed indiscriminately; leaving the reader to figure out what is truth and what is not. It is no surprise that *readers* become confused and draw the wrong conclusions. To illustrate my point, a woman has been unjustly suspected of wrongdoing as the direct result of an article of this kind printed in another local publication. We cannot stand idly by and allow this injustice to go unchallenged.

It is not unusual for a young and inexperienced reporter to allow her ambition to cloud her judgment. However, those of us who have dedicated our lives to honest and ethical journalism have a duty to make sure that we do not allow our employees to violate the standards of moral and ethical behavior that our readers expect and deserve.

"Keeping this philosophy in mind, I take pleasure in announcing a special award to be given yearly to a talented local journalist, for a story, fiction or non-fiction, which appeared in any of our local papers during the past year. It will be called 'The Louis Neuberger Award for Writing,' in memory of my late husband.

"It gives me great pleasure to present the first such award to Tanya McCullough, for her imaginative article about one of the stories entered in the Dos Hermanas Short Story Contest. Tanya, will you please come forward? You too, Mrs. McCullough."

Jean rose to her feet and, holding her daughter's hand firmly, led the way to the microphone. Tanya's normally pale face flushed a dull red and as she walked to the front of the dining room, she kept her eyes straight ahead and looked at no one.

"Thank you for coming today, Tanya and Mrs. McCullough. Please accept this certificate of award for 'creative writing in the media.

"Tanya's story about Luisa Marino's unusual tale, 'The Witch and the Engineer' is not just good writing. It is also a prime example of how a skilled writer can combine truth with fiction to create the illusion that truth and fiction are one and the same. Tanya, a staff writer for 'The Braggart,' has shown remarkable talent in this direction, but she still has much to learn.

Therefore, Tanya, I would like to extend to you an offer of a six month paid internship on the staff of "The Sentinel," where you will, I hope, polish your journalistic ability through contact with the most ethical and professional journalists in the county, if not the whole state of California. Of course, I am somewhat biased, but I trust you will forgive me for that."

Dr. Neuberger handed a beautifully embossed certificate to Tanya, and a letter confirming the internship to Jean, who came closer to the microphone and spoke.

"Dr. Neuberger, Miranda and friends, as you can see, my daughter is quite overcome by your generosity, and so I shall, with her permission, accept this generous award in her name. I am proud of her ability to write and I am delighted that she has this opportunity to learn even more in the highly professional and ethical milieu of 'The Sentinel.' On behalf of my daughter and myself, thank you and God bless you all."

As Jean and Tanya resumed their seats, the audience broke into enthusiastic applause and delighted laughter.

Most of them realized how cleverly Miranda and Dr. Neuberger had given Tanya her comeuppance. However, there were also a few who recognized the wisdom in creating the opportunity for Tanya to learn to use her gift ethically and with compassion. Would Tanya take advantage of it? No one had a clue, not even Tanya's mother.

Miranda came forward and shook Dr. Neuberger's hand warmly.

"Thank you, Barbara. And now, the moment we have all been waiting for…

Will the judges' committee please hand me the envelope?

Rabbi Moseson came forward and handed Miranda a plain white envelope.

"Thank you, Rabbi."

Miranda tore open the sealed envelope, unfolded the sheet of paper inside and smiled, as she read the name of the winner.

"The winner of the first annual Dos Hermanas Short Story Contest is none other than Dos Hermanas' own Rebecca Proudfoot for her story entitled 'Ma-Ya's Tale.' Rebecca, will you please come forward to claim your prize."

The tall attractive young author came forward, smiling broadly.

"Thank you. Thank you all!" were the only words she could muster.

"You are most welcome, my dear Rebecca. Your story was wonderful. We hope you will continue to write the stories that your people have handed down verbally from generation to generation for many years to come."

She handed Rebecca a nicely framed certificate with a colorful border of green laurel leaves, awarding her "First Place in the First Annual Dos Hermanas Short Story Contest."

"As you know, the first place winner also receives a gourmet dinner here at Miranda's Cafe for herself and her family on a date of her choice. So just reserve a date, Rebecca and we'll do the rest."

"Now we would like to award prizes to our other finalists as well. Each of you has written a story that has brought much pleasure to this audience. Our judges committee has counted the votes and you all came in within one or two votes of each other. Therefore, it was the judge's unanimous decision to declare each of you a winner in your own category. For the funniest story, it is my pleasure to award this certificate and gourmet dinner for two to Josh Roberts for his story entitled 'The Shtick."

Josh, c'mon up here by me while I announce the other winners."

Josh walked proudly up to the microphone and stood next to Miranda.

"For the most touching story, the prize goes to Emma Siegal, for her story entitled, 'Sara's Cruise.' Come on up, Mrs. Siegal and join us at the mike."

Emma, dignified as always, came to the front of the room and took her place on Miranda's other side. She accepted her certificate with a smile and a soft "Thank you."

"The winner of the eeriest tale, 'The Engineer and The Witch' is Luisa Marino. Now Luisa and her husband are still away, so we will hold her prizes until she returns."

Suddenly, a voice from the back of the room interrupted the proceedings.

"Just a moment. Miranda, if you don't mind, I'd like to say a few words."

Everyone turned around to see who had spoken.

"Mayor Greenwood," Miranda acknowledged his presence.

"This is an unexpected pleasure, Mayor, but of course you are welcome to say whatever you wish. Please come up to the microphone."

The short round-faced man, with graying red hair came forward.

"Thank you, Miranda. Before you wrap up the proceedings, I'd like to have a few words with you all. I think I know most of you and you know me. Many of you helped elect me to my position as Mayor of Dos Hermanas.

"Now, I've known Miranda and Joseph ever since they chose to make their home in Dos Hermanas and take over the old 'Dos Hermanas Diner.' After it became 'Miranda's Cafe', a wonderful thing happened: This cafe, over the years, has become the social center of our town. People around here always know where to go, not only for a good meal, but also for a friendly word, a ready ear, and pleasant companionship. Miranda's weekly story telling events have been a special pleasure, and often a way to let us know, in a subtle way, what's important.

"Once again, in initiating this story telling contest, she has shown us the way to make our town even greater than it was before. Little did Miranda and Joseph know, when they conceived the idea of having this contest, where it would lead. We certainly didn't expect our town to suffer a hate crime, perpetrated by a couple of ne'er do well skinheads. However, never let it be said that we allowed this kind of obscenity to win the day.

"Several of our fine citizens rolled up their sleeves and cleaned up the mess before you could wink three times. That's the kind of people we are here in Dos Hermanas!

"There has also been some suggestion of wrong-doing on the part of one of the contestants, based on nothing more than the story she entered in this contest. Well, as to that, as your Mayor, I must categorically state that Nurse Luisa Marino is one of the finest, most professional women it has been this town's privilege to claim as a citizen. I will do everything in my power to clear Nurse Marino of any charges of unprofessional conduct."

A burst of applause greeted the Mayor's announcement. He smiled and continued:

"But that is not enough. These events have given us fair warning. It can happen here! From now on, we must all, and I stress 'All' of us be vigilant of the subtle signs of hatred, so that we can neutralize them before they lead to hateful acts such as we have witnessed lately.

"As always, Miranda has shown us the way to make our fine community even better. Therefore, if it is all right with Miranda and Joseph, I would like to propose that we make Miranda's Annual Storytelling Contest an official Dos Hermanas Event, occurring every year at this time. How would you like it, Miranda, if we all pitched in and helped you make a tradition of the great service which you have done our town?"

He turned toward Miranda and awaited her answer. She was momentarily speechless. She walked the few steps to where the Mayor stood and nodded her acceptance of his proposition. Then she hugged him. The audience burst into loud cheers and whistles. Finally, Miranda spoke:

"Thank you, Mayor Greenwood. I am sure I also speak for Joseph when I accept your generous offer of sponsorship. Thank you all for your support and help. I love you, each and every one!"

CHAPTER THIRTEEN

Alas, Gentle Reader, the time has come to finish this tale. It is not an easy task! I have come to understand the addictive quality of creativity. I have stepped into the shoes of the Deity and created a world...a tiny one, to be sure, but a world that I rule, and that is heady wine, indeed. I think I understand now why the Eternal Author lets bad things happen. What a dull affair life would be without conflict! Only when we strive against evil, do we fulfill the role that has been written for us, the role of creatures just a little lower than the angels!

The Storysmith

* * * * * * * * *

Miranda drove her pick-up into the garage and turned off the ignition. She sat there quietly for a minute or two, and reviewed the day's events. So much had happened in this one day that it seemed to Miranda that there must have been more than the normal twenty-four hours in it. She was dog-tired, no doubt about it.

She pulled her keys out, tossed them into her purse, and got out of the driver's seat, closing the door of the little truck behind her. As she entered the house, the warmth of it engulfed her like a cozy blanket. She felt as though she could curl up like a kitten right where she stood and sleep for a week.

"I'm home!" she announced, "Where are you, Joseph?"

"In the living room," he responded, "Come and see what I've been up to."

Miranda smiled, and followed the sound of his voice. When she got to the archway into the living room, she was greeted by the sight of a merrily burning fire in the fireplace and a large tray on the coffee table. On it was a cheese board with a perfectly ripe wedge of Brie surrounded by her favorite sesame crackers.

A bowl of Jonathan and Granny Smith apples crowned with little bunches of Tokay and concord grapes sat by a clay wine cooler with an opened bottle of Johannisberg Riesling and two glasses.

"Oh, my darling, what a lovely greeting! I am so weary, I can hardly move. Come here and give me a hug and a kiss."

Joseph obeyed the welcome command and held her in his arms for a long moment before obliging her with a tender kiss and a hug.

"Welcome home, Miranda."

"Thank you. You can't imagine how good it feels to be here! Tell you what, I'm going to grab a quick bath and 'change into something more comfortable,' to coin a phrase. Then I'll be back to enjoy this marvelous feast with you…Okay?"

"Okay. Does that phrase you coined mean what I think it means?"

"I guess you'll just have to wait and see," she coquetted, and left the room.

Joseph poured himself a glass of wine and sat down in front of the fire. He gazed into the flames and savored the moment. Every now and then, it seemed to Joseph, there was a brief event that would etch itself indelibly into his psyche. It was never one of any particular importance in the scheme of things. It could be just a few seconds in which he was acutely aware of his surroundings and sensed that this moment was extraordinary. He treasured these vignettes and could recall them with all of his senses and find new joy and comfort in them every time. Almost all of them centered around the lovely woman with whom he'd chosen to spend his life.

As though his tender thought had summoned her, Miranda appeared in the arched doorway between the front entry and the living room. She had bathed and changed into a soft velour robe. Her freshly washed hair curled in damp ringlets about her face. Her little amulet of Hathor rested lightly on her breast. Her cheeks were rosy from her bath and her dark eyes smiled at him as much as her mouth did.

"Welcome back, my dear," he greeted her. "Why don't you make yourself comfortable here."

He indicated the large, soft, butterscotch suede armchair with its matching ottoman. "Warm your tootsies, while I pour you a glass of wine."

"Sounds wonderful," she responded and sank gratefully into the comfortable embrace of this, her favorite chair. She watched Joseph as he poured her wine and then set about preparing some crackers with Brie for her.

"What a sweet man you are, Joseph," she said. She waved her hand at the fire and the wine and the snack he'd prepared so carefully.

They sat quietly for a while, sipping their wine and nibbling on the fruit and cheese. Finally, Miranda set her wine glass down and turned her face from the flames to Joseph's face. "Joseph, I am perplexed."

Joseph nodded and waited for her to continue.

"We have reached the conclusion of our story contest and I still haven't a clue as to finding a successor. All of the stories were great and all of our finalists showed excellent presence and story telling technique. I'm glad I didn't have to pick the winner. I've thought about each of the finalists, Rebecca, Luisa, Josh and Emma. The first three already have careers and would have no reason to switch. Emma is too old and fragile."

"I was impressed with the treasure trove of stories and story tellers among us. I never realized we had such rich resources here in Dos Hermanas," said Joseph.

"Me either," agreed Miranda, "and that, in itself has been worth finding out. The story contest dinners have been a good idea in many ways. They've proved to be moneymakers and we should turn a modest profit when it's all been totaled up. The town spirit has been great and Mayor Greenwood's offer of sponsorship from here on will make our job easier next year, I think."

"You know, Miranda, you just don't sound like a person who is planning on retiring any time soon. Are you sure that retirement would suit you?"

"Funny you should mention it, Joseph. I guess I'd like to continue as I am for a while yet, but sooner or later, I will need to back off to a greater degree. Running the cafe is hard work and I may not be able to keep up the pace as I get older."

"Isn't that something you can deal with when and if it happens? I mean you could probably hire a manager if it came to that."

Miranda twiddled the stem of her wine glass and gazed at the fire as it started to die down a bit.

"My sense of this town is that it is important to maintain the cafe as a social and cultural gathering place. The churches are the only other social centers, and of course, religion and sect divide them. The cafe is the only place that is non-sectarian, multi-ethnic and gender equal in what it offers. Whoever runs it, it's vital that he or she share these attitudes. I feel a sense of obligation to make sure that the cafe continues as it has developed under our ownership and management."

Miranda sipped at her wine reflectively as Joseph waited for her to continue.

"The Goddess told me that I would be successful in my quest, although not in the way I expected,"

"Well, there you are, Miranda. It's probably too soon to make any decisions. Why don't you wait and let things develop a little more. You've set the wheels in motion by running this contest. Perhaps the person you seek will reveal herself next year. In the mean time, let's not 'push the river,' as the saying goes."

"Easier said than done, Joseph," Miranda chuckled. "Patience is not my forte…Now, how about another glass of this delicious wine?"

"My pleasure," said Joseph.

* * * * * * * * *

Miranda turned the flame down under the enormous iron kettle of lamb stew that she had prepared for her dinner patrons.

"While the stew is simmering Ruthie, would you mind preparing the veggies? We'll add them later, so they don't get too mushy."

"Let's see now, you'll be wanting carrots, pearl onions, potatoes and rutabagas. Isn't that right, Miranda?" asked Ruthie.

"Yes, but we'll cook the rutabagas separately, so they don't overpower the stew. We'll mash them with butter and nutmeg and serve them as an accompaniment with the stew."

Ruthie nodded. "Lamb stew is a lovely thing on a winter's night and it smells just wonderful."

"With a loaf of crusty bread to sop up the gravy and a glass of good red table wine, it's one of my favorite meals," replied Miranda. "It's a marvel one doesn't see it on the menus of more restaurants. I think we'll offer a 'special' tonight: …one price for the stew, a glass of red wine and some crusty rolls on the table."

Ruthie nodded her agreement and began to prepare the vegetables. Miranda went into the dining room to make sure the service table had a good supply of silverware and napkins.

Just then, Melanie opened the front door and entered the cafe. She was carrying the evening newspaper and the latest edition of "The Penny Saver", a shopping throwaway.

"Hi Miranda, I just picked these up off the front sidewalk; where do you want them?"

"Right next to the cash register will be fine, Melanie. Aren't you rather early, Mel? You're not due in for another half hour yet."

"Uh-huh. I was hoping you'd have a few minutes to listen to something I wrote for my creative writing assignment. It's about you and the cafe, so Mom suggested that I get your 'okay' before presenting it to my class."

"I appreciate that, Mel. It's pretty quiet right now and people won't start coming in for early dinners until about five o'clock, so let's do it now. C'mon back into the kitchen and Ruthie can listen, too. Is that okay with you?"

"Sure. I'll stow my books and hang up my sweater and be with you in just a minute."

Melanie followed Miranda into the kitchen. Ruthie was busy cutting up vegetables for the stew, so Miranda picked up a paring knife and began to peel the potatoes.

Melanie selected a manila folder from her backpack and settled herself on a kitchen stool. She opened the folder and removed several pages. When she was ready, she cleared her throat and began to read aloud.

"Once, in a small town in northern California, a woman named 'Miranda' ran a cafe appropriately named 'Miranda's Cafe.' Most of the people who came to her cafe would tell themselves that they came for the delicious food Miranda prepared, but it was really the stories that Miranda told that had captured their attention."

Melanie had begun somewhat shyly, but as she continued, her voice picked up strength and volume. Miranda could feel herself being drawn in by Melanie's clear alto voice. There was a depth and complexity to the timbre that Miranda couldn't define, but it was a compelling sound. This was not a shy and awkward child reading to her, but a self assured young woman who could, and would command attention with her presence.

"No one knew exactly how she did it, but the words she chose, the remarkable speaking voice, the tales she had composed completely enthralled them."

Ruthie and Miranda stood, paring knives still in their hands, and listened open-mouthed as Melanie continued to read, unaware of the effect she was having on her audience.

"'Once,' she began, 'before the earth was even thought of, there was a magic place, loved by the Goddess, where joy and peace, laughter and loving kindness ruled supreme.' As she went on describing each flower that grew there, roses and lilies, forget-me-nots and fragrant lavender, and each creature that lived there her listeners would find their cares dropping away from them like dead leaves in autumn. With each shining word, they would feel the lightness of spirit that made living such fun when they were children.'"

Miranda glanced over at Ruthie and the two women looked meaningfully into each other's eyes with raised eyebrows. An almost imperceptible nod passed between them. They caught each other's meaning without a word: Is this the person we've been searching for?

Miranda slowly lifted one finger to her lips, indicating, "Don't say anything to Mel about this right now."

Ruthie nodded her understanding. Melanie continued reading, unaware of the effect she was having.

"Often, Miranda would tell of strange and comical creatures: 'The ouroboros is a worm,' she would explain, 'who has the unique compulsion to swallow his own tail. Thus he spends his entire life going in smaller and smaller circles, devouring himself through all eternity.' They chuckled at the impossible picture this created for them, but some felt a little uncomfortable as well; they sensed a subtle message in Miranda's story, if only they were wise enough to understand it. Her voice would caress and comfort some

among them; for others, there was a sense of gentle irony, although they could not be sure if it applied to them.

"Sometimes, however, there was a soaring sense of freedom that gave some folks the courage to tackle seemingly impossible tasks."

Melanie looked up into Miranda's eyes and smiled. Miranda returned the smile, but she could feel the tears welling up as Melanie's lovely voice told of the wonderful effect that Miranda's stories had on her life.

"All at once, they found that they possessed the ability to complete them successfully. The pleasure of this enraptured them, and they blessed Miranda's soul each time that they prayed."

There was a moment of absolute stillness as Miranda and Ruthie realized how special Mel's story was. It was as if Melanie had opened her soul to them and they could, at last, see the beauty and the talent that lay hidden beneath Melanie's diffident manner.

At that moment, the front door bell announced the arrival of a patron.

"There's more," said Melanie, "It's all about the contest and what's been happening here, but I can read it to you later, if you want me to."

"Oh my dear Melanie, what a beautiful story! Please don't change a word of it…and your reading is exceptional! I can hardly wait to hear the rest of it."

Miranda went over to Melanie and took the sweet face in her hands. She kissed Melanie gently on the forehead and then hugged her warmly.

"I signed this piece 'The Storysmith'," said Melanie, "Do you think that's okay? I mean it's not too pretentious, is it?"

"No., I think it's perfect!" said Miranda, "and I think you should use it for every story you write!"

* * * * * * * * *

The last patron, a rough-hewn man with work-worn fingers, had finished and paid for his dinner. As Miranda brought him his change, he commented, "It's been years since I tasted a lamb stew as good as this one…not since my mother, God rest her soul, passed away.

"I'm happy to hear you liked it," answered Miranda. It's one of my favorites, too."

She saw him to the door and after they had bid each other "Good-bye." she closed and locked the door behind him. Turning the "Open" sign around so that "Closed" showed from the outside of the cafe, Miranda gathered up the tray of dirty dishes and carried them into the kitchen. Ruthie was sitting on a stool, and had propped her foot up on an upended milk crate. She was sipping a cup of chamomile tea and nibbling on a Graham cracker. After Miranda had added the dishes to the last load in the dishwasher, and pressed the "on" button, she turned to Ruthie.

"Ruthie, my dear, is your leg bothering you?"

"Just a bit. It does tend to swell if I've been on my feet over-long."

"Are you sure it's okay for you to be working so soon after the accident? As glad as I am that you're back, the last thing in the world I'd want is for you to hurt yourself."

"To tell you the truth, Miranda, my darlin', it is a bit hard on me. I'm not as young or strong as I used to be, and

I've been thinking for some time now about cutting back to part-time."

"I can understand that," responded Miranda.

"Well, Miranda, you know I'd never leave you in the lurch. So, the other day when Irene was in, I took the liberty of talking it over with her."

"Yes?" prompted Miranda.

"Uh-huh, and between the two of us, we came up with a plan. What would you say to Irene continuing to work here part-time? Then I could plan my schedule around her teaching schedule, and you'd have at least one of us here at all times, not to mention Danny and Melanie."

"Did Irene say she wanted to stay on here?" asked Miranda.

"Oh, my darlin', she loves the work especially when folks compliment her cooking, and the extra money she earns comes in mighty handy with two children in college at the same time. Irene would be thrilled to stay on, if it suits you, Miranda."

"It suits me just fine, Ruthie…You know, I think I see a pattern here. It doesn't seem as though you and I will retire any time soon, but when we do, it looks like this operation will remain a family affair."

"If you're talking about Irene's family, I think you're right," said Ruthie. "How do you suppose it will happen?"

"I haven't got a clue, Ruthie, but happen it will! I don't know how or when, but this I do know: "Sometimes you have to let a story write its own ending."

* * * * * * * * *

The First Annual Dos Hermanas Short Story Contest was over, and the townsfolk turned their attention to the approaching holidays. A new year was fast approaching, and even more exciting, a new millennium! What would the year 2000 bring to Dos Hermanas?

Normally, the local folks took comfort in the thought that "nothing ever happens in Dos Hermanas." But this year had been different, thanks to Miranda and the contest. One of Dos Hermanas' most beloved citizens was suspected of being a witch and was undergoing an investigation of her background! "Skinheads" had graffitied hate messages all over Miranda's Cafe and practically accused her of changing herself into a ravening wolf! A clarion call had been sounded and the good citizens of our town had rallied to the cause of common decency and the spirit of helping one's neighbors, by painting over the disgusting epithets on the walls of the cafe!

However, there was still some unfinished business to be attended to: Nurse Luisa Marino was still under investigation concerning allegations that she used witchcraft in her work as neonatal nursery supervisor. Miranda had dealt with Tanya McCullough by awarding her a prize for fiction in the local media, which, in effect, accused her of lying, but gave her the opportunity of learning about ethical Journalism through a paid internship on a highly respected newspaper. Would she act on it? Last, but not least, would there be a Second Annual Dos Hermanas Short Story Contest?

On a personal note, when I decided to tell the story of the story contest, I had no idea it would have such a significant effect on me. As I think back on the events of the last few months, I feel something like a "reverse ouroboros". Rather than swallowing my tail, like the mythical creature in Miranda's stories however, I have discovered more and more of myself as I described each of the winning short stories, as well as all the true events that came about because of Miranda's deep commitment to this community and all its people.

Life happens in short increments, and whether we call them "events" or "stories" matters little. Sometimes, they have an extraordinary effect on the people involved. That certainly holds true for me! I can think of no better life than to write stories and share them with others, as Miranda has done. Perhaps, some day, I will be able to have such a life.

Sincerely,
Melanie Schoenberg
The Storysmith

ABOUT THE AUTHOR

Arlene Spector was born in the Bronx, New York and educated at N.Y.U. In 1955, she married Murray Spector, from Brooklyn. She taught school for two years until motherhood intervened.

Later, she became a career counselor and co-founder of The Women's Career Center at Middlesex College, where she developed seminars in effective communication skills for local corporations including IBM, Union Carbide, and Johnson and Johnson.

Arlene's poetry has been published in three anthologies. Her one-woman poetry reading attracted an overflow crowd.

Arlene and her husband now live in San Pedro, California, where she learned to laugh at herself and the lunatic world around her. She brings her perceptive, humorous, quirky view of reality to us in this, her first novel…ENJOY!

Printed in the United States
779600002B